BOA
EDITIONS LTD

TO ASSUME A PLEASING SHAPE

TO ASSUME
A PLEASING
SHAPE

STORIES BY JOSEPH SALVATORE

AMERICAN READER SERIES, NO. 16

BOA Editions, Ltd. ❖ Rochester, NY ❖ 2011

First Edition
11 12 13 14   7 6 5 4 3 2 1

For information about permission to reuse any material from this book please contact The Permissions Company at www.permissionscompany.com or e-mail permdude@eclipse.net.

Publications by BOA Editions, Ltd.—a not-for-profit corporation under section 501 (c) (3) of the United States Internal Revenue Code—are made possible with funds from a variety of sources, including public funds from the New York State Council on the Arts, a state agency; the Literature Program of the National Endowment for the Arts; the County of Monroe, NY; the Lannan Foundation for support of the Lannan Translations Selection Series; the Mary S. Mulligan Charitable Trust; the Rochester Area Community Foundation; the Arts & Cultural Council for Greater Rochester; the Steeple-Jack Fund; the Ames-Amzalak Memorial Trust in memory of Henry

ART WORKS.
arts.gov

State of the Arts

NYSCA

Ames, Semon Amzalak and Dan Amzalak; and contributions from many individuals nationwide. See Colophon on page 128 for special individual acknowledgments.

Cover Design: Sandy Knight
Interior Design and Composition: Richard Foerster
Manufacturing: McNaughton & Gunn
BOA Logo: Mirko

Library of Congress Cataloging-in-Publication Data

Salvatore, Joseph.
   To assume a pleasing shape : stories / by Joseph Salvatore. — 1st ed.
      p. cm. — (American readers series ; no. 16)
   ISBN 978-1-934414-55-2
   I. Title.
   PS3619.A44253T7 2011
   813'.6—dc22

2011001430

BOA Editions, Ltd.
250 North Goodman Street, Suite 306
Rochester, NY 14607
www.boaeditions.org
A. Poulin, Jr., Founder (1938–1996)

Contents

For my mother, my first reader.

And to the memory of my father.

There is but one animal. . . . An animal is an entity taking its shape, or rather its different shapes, from the environment in which it develops. Zoological species are the result. . . . I saw that in these regards society resembled Nature.

—Balzac, forward to *The Human Comedy*, 1842

"Then what would be the purpose *of possession?" Karras said, frowning. "What's the point?"*

"Who can know?" answered Merrin. "Who can really hope to know? . . . I think the demon's target is not the possessed; it is us . . . the observers . . . every person in this house. And I think—I think the point is to make us despair; to reject our own humanity, Damien: to see ourselves as ultimately bestial; as ultimately vile and putrescent; without dignity; ugly; unworthy. And there lies the heart of it, perhaps: in unworthiness."

—William Peter Blatty, *The Exorcist*, 1971

Anthropologists have begun to decipher the mysterious physical behaviors of possession. They suggest that the possessed disengage themselves from "the socially constructed world of everyday life" and enter a state in which what is deemed socially dangerous within their psyche is allowed freer reign. . . . With no legitimate way to express this conflict directly, the unbearable psychic tensions are expressed physically—through women's bodies.

—Carol F. Karlsen, *The Devil in the Shape of a Woman*, 1987

Parts

Well, when I used to get to fretting about it, my daddy (now dead) used to say that really the only thing left to say about the human body is it's composed of parts, known and unknown. Them's all there is to it, he used to say. And here he weren't speaking solely of the organs wherein hides the diseases we can't be sure of or the ailments we can't barely name (and rest assured, he used to say, there are many of those; never knowing then, poor man, how right he was). Rather my daddy (no longer with us) would soothe my fretting about his news by speaking of the stuff that fires the furnace of the human spirit. He was a great one for that. Always talking this and that fuss about the human spirit. Especially that last year, when he'd take me apprenticing with him. A good cup of coffee, he'd say, sliding his hammer back into his belt, and a half-full breakfast (used to stress "half-full") can keep a human body moving till about midday, then you gotta get a light little lunch into you (used to stress "light"), maybe a touch more coffee, followed later by a lean dinner (used to stress "lean"), then even later, if you want, a bit of alcohol, sure—some beer, some wine, what have you, something to help you relax, followed by a good night's sleep; and then why you and your body and your spirit be good to go another day. But the thing is, he used to say, running his eye down a length of pine, you gotta keep doing that over the course of a lifetime. You can't stop. Gotta keep fueling that furnace. Somehow find a way. You'll get some money. Some wife. Some kids. A boy of your own, maybe. A house, a pet or two. A collection of stuff in a garage, a cellar, an attic. And then but soon another thing you get is breakdown. The innards, my late daddy meant. They can't keep it up. Spirit and spine—well shit, he'd say, a good cup of coffee handle that. But the innards. . . . Never forget, they the reason we say everything comes to an end. Because them's all the known. We *know* that shit dies. That shit starts dying the day you're born. And as much as we know how to keep it going, we don't know how we keep going till that shit dies—that's great mystery to folks like you and me, he used to say, lifting me into the passenger side of his pickup, throwing his tool belt in beside me, pushing the door-lock down before slamming shut that door. How we keep pouring them cups of coffee, caring to retrieve such fuel, all when we gonna need to do it again and again and again until that day we can't, he'd say, his hand on the wheel, shaking a little, I remember; the start of them tremors. How we manage to do it over and over again, he'd say, knowing what all we know and all we don't; how we gotta look our boys straight in the eye and tell them this whole truth—well, them's the great unknowns, he used to say. Them's the hard parts.

Reduction

I. Eyes Fell Down Her Face

The woman hated her own breasts, a hatred directed not merely toward their size, but to *the very fact* of them, the fact that she *had* these breasts, the responsibility and mandate of having to deal and cope with having breasts of this size, deal and cope with all the objective and subjective responses a society, culture, patriarchy might have toward a person with this-sized breasts, the kind of breasts that drew eyes like divining rods to earth-covered wells. The eyes of men—and women—on the subway, on Fifth Avenue, in the park on her way to class, in the stacks at Bobst, at Washington Mews, in the Ireland House, at faculty meetings, academic conferences, student advising appointments, committee meetings, curriculum-planning meetings, co-op board meetings, political rallies, protest marches, in waiting rooms, restaurants, laundromats, coffee shops, in the city, in the suburbs, on the beaches of Marblehead, in Salem's Peabody Essex Museum doing research on the Witch Trials, at the movies, at the ballet, even *The Nutcracker*, at home or abroad, here, there, everywhere, a globalism of gaze. For wherever she went, since the age of sixteen, eyes fell down her face. Even the eyes of her female students in her *House(frau)keeping: Representations of Post-Feminist Identities in U.S. Suburbs* class. Even in her *Cult of (the) Madonna* course last fall, as well as her *Crone's Disease: Witches, Mid-Wives, and America's Contempt for Female Non-Normative Behavior* course.

Sometimes she'd look up after reading aloud from the Butler or the Halberstam and encounter her female students' eyes rapt, cast up from their desks at her torso, pens poised before parted lips. And the men she'd slept with—always most interested in the moment the bra came off, helpful as could be with the unfastening, the lowering of straps, the swift pulling-off of that tight harness, anything to get them out for viewing. That rapturous moment when the bra would finally be off—you could see it in their faces: revelation, wonder, awe. But everything post-bra: quotidian. (The man in her life was a bit of an exception. She'd seen that look in his eyes early on, but he soon figured it out, remembered the woman attached. He was a man, after all, a good man—chair of her anthro department, a specialist in global masculinities, his book, *Finding Our Fathers: A Man's Journey Home*, resting at number three on the *Times* best-seller list for thirteen weeks, a half-hour slot on *Fresh Air*—but still only a man.) She had an irrational fear (which she knew to be just that, due in large part to her weekly sessions with Barbara on Central Park West) of what a surgeon or an O.R. assistant might think or say, or how he might wince or make momentary eye-contact with the other attending male surgeons if one or both of her breasts ever had to be removed. She imagined the light-blue torso twist of the surgical-masked assistant as the heavy, now womanless breast was handed off to be placed in a hazmat bag, the men with their hairy forearms in the O.R. repressing the urge to say something or flinch (as a totally natural response to the indescribable stress that occurs in the O.R., which stress she understood from regular viewing of the medical

drama, *Grey's Anatomy*), just some barely noticeable but utterly present O.R. tension-relieving reaction to the hefty
breast, avec tumor, sans woman.

There had been another detached breast dream last
spring in San Francisco while attending an American Studies conference. The night before she was to present her paper, she watched the aforementioned medical drama on her
hotel room's big TV, her laptop and BlackBerry and yellow
legal pads and pink and purple Post-its and gender theory
texts strewn like stuffed animals all over the bed; the two
sweaters and one turtleneck and blouse and vest and blazer
and silk scarf and two sports bras she had planned to wear
for tomorrow's talk hanging in the closet. In her nightmare,
a handsome surgeon pulled down his mask and lifted with
both hands her freshly mastectomied breast's nipple to his
mouth and sucked three times like a baby, lifting his eyes
and eyebrows simultaneously on each of the three sucks
to meet the eyes of the three attending male surgeons, all
huddled bluely over her anesthetized and gaze-deserted
and breastless body.

That raw tearing-out from the O.R. back to her hotel
room when something loud in the hallway woke her was
unbearable to endure alone. She called the man, but his
cell phone must have been turned off. Lying in the dark,
naked, she could still see the mastectomied breast, the
dark, serrated dripping oval of its severing, its wet wires
and circuits of clipped veins and mucusy tissue; and, when,
after taking three Xanaxes with a small bottle of wine from
her hotel room's minibar, she fell back to sleep, the dream
reanimated and there again was the severed breast in the
man's hands, and with each of the man's sucks, she could see
the tumor itself begin to push its way through the mucus,
extruding itself from the morass of gore as though it were
alive, like the head of some creature crowning, struggling

to be born. That morning in the shower, after coffee and two more Xanaxes, she felt for lumps.

But there were no lumps. There were never any lumps—despite the aggressive self-exams she regularly administered—not even a family history.

And so because she could not have her breasts removed (she wasn't insane, after all, just depressed and weary and gaze-sickened, especially after reading in the *Post* about a woman in Australia who'd experienced such a crippling phobia of her own E-cupped breasts that she tried to trick a doctor into removing them both; the Australian woman was arrested for insurance fraud and later committed suicide), did not, in fact, even want them removed, but, rather, wanted them never to have existed at all, she opted instead, with Barbara's support, to push through her irrational fear of surgery and have her breasts reduced, diminishing the load she could no longer bear, and thus diminishing, she hoped, her complicated, secret loathing—not a despising of the feminine or any gender-betrayal or some terribly difficult gender-identity confusion, but rather a hatred directed toward the unthinkable: The woman hated the shape of her breasts, not merely their size and the fact of their being attached to her, but *their very shape*, the sense that the shape was hegemonic within its bodily borders, tyrannical over her own self-image and her appearance to others and her way in the world, their very shape oppressing her. For they were to her mind not breasts at all, but gigantic blob-sacks—humongous, blunt, long, doughy, fat, flabby, blue-lightening-veined slabs—large in the wrong way, floppy in a sickening way, the very *way* of them reminding her of those stitched-leather speed-bags that boxers wallop back and forth. Cumbrous and mastodonic and lubberly and horrible and hanging and floppy and whopping and utterly slablike. More like someone's huge fat thigh than a breast. Her chiropractor, Dr. Richard Stiglioni of Union Square East, and her psychotherapist, Dr. Barbara Stein of Central Park West, both, in their effort to validate her feelings, acknowledged that her breasts were indeed large and indeed heavy, and that their stress on her lower back and the accompanying frustration and weariness of having to heft that weight every day was, no doubt, a tremendous strain on the woman's spine and spirit.

And so the woman hated her breasts (although, not always: once, on a beach in Florida, in the 1980s, on spring break, she was demolishedly drunk and got talked into entering a wet-T-shirt contest, indisputably winning the minute the water was thrown over her, the other contestants, no doubt bitter, remarking that the woman's breasts could be used as flotation devices and/or beach balls; but her victory had to do with more than her breasts, she knew: for she was thin-waisted and curvy-hipped and long-limbed and bosomy and tall, standing on that open-air collapsible stage, holding up her long auburn hair with one hand, shaking her chest now in a way she had only ever before done in private, alone before her mirror, unashamed now, playful even—what happened to that young woman? she sometimes wondered), her hatred further complicated by the fact that hating her breasts for being merely large and heavy and misshapen implied her ratification of an ideal of the perfect breast, a beauty myth that was no doubt instilled in her at a precritical, preconscious age by a patriarchal, culturally constructed norm of the perfect platonic breast—platonically large, but not Homerically mammoth—that the world had decided was the perfect breast. A breast that advertisers and American consumers preferred. Like girls in *Shape* magazine had. Like her classmates at Barnard had had. Like women at the gym had.

Yet what the woman secretly feared, when she came right down to it, what she hated most viciously, resented most bitterly, was the fact that unlike runway models with their prepubescent-boy-body's flat A-cupped chests, or sporty young women with their firm B-cupped apples, pert nipples like little stems, what the woman feared and loathed about her resentment and loathing most was that her breasts were ugly, their ugliness magnified by their monstrous size. And, in her darkest moments, there was the flickering thought that her breasts made her look—*no, no, no*, she couldn't admit it even to herself, the truth was too hideously perverse—the woman hated herself for hating her breasts because sometimes, if she happened to be feeling particularly sensitive to the culture's criticism and sexist mind-control, or found herself vulnerable on certain anxious, low-self-esteem-ridden, drinking-deep-of-the-culture's-Kool-Aid days, the woman feared that her breasts made her *look fat*. And then it seemed she was nothing more than a fat pair of monstrous breasts walking through the world. How her female colleagues at the university would despise her, she well knew, if they were ever to discover her traitorous breast-loathing.

II. MIMESIS & MASCULINITY & METAPHOR & METONYMY & ON & ON & ON &, &, &, &

The man in her life wanted to be a man for her. He wanted to fix her broken situation because of his feelings for the woman, which were to his mind *loving*. But, as a cultural anthropologist (Why be modest? He was the head of the largest and most well-funded anthropology department in lower Manhattan), he was also acutely and painfully aware that his wanting to help the woman made him guilty of reinforcing the very system that had led to her confusion and low self-esteem and breast-loathing in the first place. He agreed with Kaminer (1992) in her critique of our society's self-help culture. He believed that the woman's psychotherapy sessions were only the playing out of a bourgeois solipsism, which enacted a consumer's complicit participation in a commercialized system that reinforced the very attitudes and norms it claimed so nobly it sought to "cure." And yet, despite his vehemence on this point, the man also acknowledged that, though he averred that one needn't "have therapy" (that *horrid* idiom) for someone to tell you how screwed up you were about not feeling "beautiful," it was nonetheless true that all humans were victim to culturally indoctrinated and reinforced notions of self-loathing; he knew, in other words, that the woman was hurting. And, regardless of his hard-line position on the self-help culture's creation of victims and whiners, it hurt him to understand this about the woman.

But she had made him understand.

She had sat him down just last night, after the anthro department's Third Friday of the Month Dinner and Public Lecture Series, where the woman had given a lecture entitled "*Madonna War Complex: Lindy Englund and America's Attitude toward Female Warriors.*" When the man and the woman had returned to their co-op, she'd invited him to sit next to her on the sofa, and then, turning to face him, said she was considering surgery to reduce the size of her breasts, and that she'd had a consultation with a doctor weeks earlier, and that, after waiting for the results of her tests, the doctor had just, that very evening, left a message on her BlackBerry saying he could have a bed ready for her on Monday morning.

The man's first reaction was interior: amazement and disbelief—why, he thought, would the woman want to have anyone cut and remove parts of her body? Especially her breasts. Which the man adored and regarded as a significant source of sexual stimulation. And if he could get really honest with himself, there was also some part of him that resented the woman for deciding—without consulting him on his feelings—to reduce the very things that provided him some little bit of pleasure in this pleasure-shaming, Puritanical, body-despising culture. But it was abundantly clear to the man in the same instant that he was being selfish and piggish and masculine and grotesque.

Thus his first exterior reaction was simply to take and hold the woman's wedding-ringless hand and listen to her, fully aware from the Tannen (1990) that men's first reaction to a woman sharing difficult feelings was to immediately rush in with advice and problem-solving rhetoric. He held her hand, and that contact made him forget himself for the minute and forget the Tannen and the fact that he was right in not wanting her to do this and she was wrong. But even before the woman's honest and difficult and emotionally-vulnerablizing disclosure, the man had, for a long while, plainly seen that the woman loathed her breasts. The way she kept them covered, layers of sweaters and jackets and blouses upon blouses and that horrid vest; the bra she wore that could flatten a medicine ball to the size of a student response paper; the way she slept naked but always held blankets under her chin. The way she covered her naked self when she rose from bed to go to the bathroom or to get a glass of water or even to get another blanket to cover her doubly. The man had tried many subtle strategies to take this shame from the woman—e.g., doing his absolute damnedest, last spring, not to let her catch him looking even once at her breasts, which avoidance strategy failed horribly within a week, as the man became obsessed with stealing furtive glances at the breasts, waiting for the moment mid-conversation when her eyes would look away from his for just a "split-second," as she tried to refocus or gather her thoughts, and in that sliver of time the man would glance down quickly at her chest and then just as quickly back up at her eyes, trying to regain and assume the same expression he'd had when she looked away, discovering that a semi-frown and knotted-brow with wider-than-usual-eyes was the easiest expression to regain after a furtive chest glance. And so within one ten minute conversation he would furtively glance down and then back up every time she looked away, at least thirty, thirty-five times, not able to hear what she was saying, but nodding earnestly nonetheless. The man became convinced that his need to look furtively and repeatedly at her breasts came as a result of trying his absolute damnedest not to. So he tried the opposite, to look at them frankly and forthrightly, without objectifying lust, gazing at them as though he were looking at the University provost's target enrollment and student retention memo. Nor did this failed attempt to appear erotically disinterested in her breasts help the woman: e.g, the week last summer when they were vacationing on the Cape, and had sex several times, the man never once touching or putting his mouth to her breasts, but rubbing or kissing her shoulders instead. Until finally she asked him if he disliked her breasts, which led to his spending the rest of their vacation dutifully attentive to her breasts, which attention neither of them, he knew, quite accepted as genuine. Nothing seemed to convince the woman that she needn't feel ashamed or morbidly self-conscious of her body. And nothing the man did seemed to help.

Truth be told, the man was all too aware that it was precisely his need to "fix" her broken situation, to "save" her because he "loved" her, that was the problem. A problem further compounded by the fact that he knew he was not so much guilty of actually feeling this way, but was, rather, *culturally conditioned* to react this way. To want to save her and be a man for her. And that knowledge terrified and disturbed the man because it made him question the one thing he felt was true and good in his life: his love feelings for the woman.

Under the sway of those love feelings, he wanted the woman to keep her extremely large breasts exactly as they were, not for his own pleasure, but for her sanity and sense of self; he wanted to eradicate her culturally conditioned hatred of her body. But it was precisely his wanting to make the woman secure with her body and feel that she was "good enough just the way she was," that made him worry he was guilty of being just another example of a patriarchally, culturally privileged man wanting to "fix" the pedestalized woman's problem, content in his privileged luxury to actually feel that it was his entitled right to "rescue" her, and, thus, by not only attempting to rescue her, but also feeling that it was in his privileged masculine power indeed *to* rescue her, he would be enacting and reinforcing the very cultural conditioning that was responsible for her hatred of herself in the first place.

The man felt despair at ever being a man for the woman in such a smoldering circular ruin as was this culture.

Now—lying naked in bed with the woman less than twenty-four hours since her revelation that she was considering breast reduction surgery this very Monday, two days hence—the man felt anxiety about some very confusing feelings he was having for the woman's breasts, anxiety compounded by the fact that he was experiencing these confusing feelings the very day after she had openly shared with him her own confusion about and loathing for her breasts. It sickened and depressed him to have such feelings. But these feelings—the man had to reassure himself—were to be expected. He was experiencing helplessness, and as the current research clearly demonstrated, that is one of the most emotionally vulnerable places a man in this society can be (Sullivan, Perth, Silverstein, 1981, 1985, 1999). He was desperate and panicky and losing his erection.

She had taken him, after their dinner tonight, by the hand from the living room couch on which she had only yesterday broken the news about her breasts, and from that site of honesty and self-disclosure and hand-holding and shared tears, had led him into the bedroom and pushed him onto their bed and said that she wanted to drip hot candle wax on his chest. The effect on the man's phallus was so swift that it drew blood from his head. She carefully unbuttoned his shirt, slid it down his arms and off his body as the man sat on the bed blinking and trying to stay upright. And then, sensitive to his self-disclosed obsessive-compulsive sartorial tendencies, she walked it to the closet and hung it up. Turning from the closet to face him, as though this were some bourgeois softcore porn fantasy, she told the man to get undressed, and then excused herself to the bathroom. When the woman returned, she strolled naked across the room, without shame or bathrobe or blanket or afghan or one of his shirts, shoulders back, breasts present and accounted for, to retrieve the long red candle from the top of the tall chest of drawers. She stood naked to light the match and touch it to the wick and then placed the taper for a moment on the trunk at the foot of the bed.

When the man looked up from where he lay, hard as a bar of pig iron, in order to gaze at the woman bending to set down the lighted candle, he saw in the candlelight the woman's breasts sway forward and flatten out and flop, while also hanging conically and somewhat slablike, swaying back and forth like twin pendulum weights inside a grandfather clock. And what came unbidden to the man's mind was the word "teat." And all at once he envisioned a cow's milk-dripping teats—the bloated and veiny pink udder, the dugs—and he became horribly aware of his raw nakedness on the bed. His thin, nearly hairless shins; his soft belly; the baby toe on his left foot missing, something the doctor attributed to his mother's heavy drinking. The man knew then that he was not a good man for the woman. He never would be. He wanted to fix her and build her up and then reduce her to a barnyard creature. And then an immediate follow-up thought brought with it a flash of anger and outrage, that his momentary comparison of her breasts with a cow's teats had to be culturally conditioned in him, something having to do with the word "tits." And this awareness of his motherfucking cultural conditioning—along with the attendant guilt and confusion and frustration and, frankly, momentary revulsion for the word "teats" after gazing at the woman's actual "tits"—this onslaught of awareness, he now feared, hating himself for thinking it, was seriously affecting the blood-flow to his erection.

III. Eyes Had Taken Her In

The woman who sought a breast reduction had indeed hated her own breasts, it's true; but tonight she was feeling complicated and ambivalent feelings regarding them. For in a few day's time, she would have them surgically reduced, the base of the breasts slit open and cut perpendicularly up toward the nipple, her nipple then scalpeled circularly and placed on ice, her breasts then spread open and clamped back, the fat tissue sucked out, parts of the mammary cut away, the nipple then taken off ice and replaced higher on the gland to account for the reshaping and remapping of her entire chest. When the doctor explained what would happen in surgery, the woman felt faint, a feeling she in-

stantly chastised herself for, aware as she was of the clichéd
tendency attributed to women to faint in doctor's offices.
But, despite that awareness, she didn't think she could go
through with it.

Her nipples had felt hot and tingly as the doctor explained the procedure and continued with the consultation. When she told him, no, she wasn't married and did
not plan on having children, he said, good, because she'd
never be able to breastfeed once the procedure was done.
He took blood and urine and her pulse, asking about family
history of cardiovascular disease, told her to put her shirt
back on and then he and the female nurse who'd observed
the whole consultation stood to leave the room. But not
before the nurse took one last surreptitious glance at her
breasts. It could have been something related to her job or
to the possible surgery, but the woman saw the look, rec-
ognized the gaze. The nurse looked up from her chest and
their eyes met. They both knew.

Last night, after she'd presented her paper at the Third
Friday lecture, her BlackBerry vibrated in her blazer pocket,
and she knew it was the doctor. And she knew now she would
overcome her irrational fear of surgery and surgeons and
go ahead and get it done. (Well, truth be told, she could not
have made this decision without extra sessions with Barbara
on Tuesday and Thursday.) And sharing all this with the
man had made her even more secure in her decision. For
the man had reached out and taken her hand and held it and
listened intently and kept his eyes focused on her and even
teared up at one moment, the exact moment she'd teared
up. There was no judgment in his eyes. And this intimacy,
which she alone initiated and controlled, empowered the
woman and made her feel closer to the man and more trust-
ing and playful and, surprisingly, somewhat aroused, and
for the first time in several months, refreshingly horny.

And yet, despite her self-awareness and feelings of empowerment and control over her life and body, and full acceptance that her decision was based on her own feelings and not the man's, there was, nonetheless, also a competing and coexistent gnawing awareness that she was falling victim to the misogynistic standards of beauty hegemonically programmed and reinforced in her by a cultural beauty myth and patriarchal notion of what the perfect breast should be. And this made the woman depressed and sick inside and throat-constricted and confused as to what she should do regarding the cutting and slitting and nipple remapping and reduction.

The feelings of sexual arousal aroused by her open sharing and disclosure were nonetheless, despite her soul sickness at her decision, still present today, waning when she graded papers in her study while the man read the first Saturday supplements of the Sunday *Times*, but refreshed when she focused on the thought she'd had when she woke up—that tonight she wanted to play with pain. Wanted to do this thing she'd seen in a movie, this thing that Madonna had done to Willem Defoe. For the woman had often let her fingers play with hot wet wax, whether at dinner or around the small table in their dining alcove; she would act as though she were listening to her dining partner, and let her fingers distractedly venture toward the candle, closing her eyes ever so imperceptibly as she felt the burn. As a little girl her father had taught her and her sister to make candles in the beach sand at night, their small house behind them as dark and indiscernible as the dunes nearly obscuring it from sight, taught her and her sister to dig little holes with their pruned fingers, and then he would pour hot wax into the little holes, and lower into that puddle a wick, and with his Zippo ignite each wick and cover it with a Mason

jar, until all over their small patch of beach little flowers
of fire flickered and waved, bits of stars in the dark sand,
lambent and strange, the lights of Nahant and Revere and
Winthrop glittering offshore, and farther south the Back
Bay glowing on the horizon way out across the dark water.
The smell of the sea; her father's cigarette smoke; the fish
stench from gull-picked shells, day-old suntan lotion still
sweet on their salty shoulders. And later when the woman
returned from college and she and her sister and mother
went to that patch of beach to let go his ashes into the vast
Atlantic, and after they made his sand candles and sat on
the driftwood log and drank red wine and dug their toes
into the moist, cold sand, the woman put a fingertip into
the puddle of wax next to her foot and raised it up in the
dark and her face felt tingly and her hair charged and she
said softly *phew, phew, phew* as she blew on the wax, the deli-
cious pain driving her crazy, but taking all else from her
mind. It was bracing in a way she'd never experienced before. Her eyes had never felt so wide.

The woman was fully aware that wanting to do the thing
she'd seen Madonna do in the film was the most problematic and obvious Platonic remove, life imitating art and all
that. And when she was grading her students' papers and
thought about enacting that filmic cliché, the woman lost
her feeling of arousal, but each time she concentrated on
the feeling of the fire, she regained a certain excitation,
the anticipation of that pain.

She would do it to the man, and then have the man
do it to her. It would be the last time she would make love
to the man with these breasts, she knew. The doctor said
there was a good chance that much of the sensation would
be lost. Tonight, she wanted to control the pain, before the
pain was out of her control; she wanted to control how she
felt. She wanted to feel what these breasts really felt like,

for the last time, without any self-consciousness. Which self-consciousness, the woman knew, would kill the mood like a motherfucker.

IV. Masculinity & Male Dominance & Mirror Stage & Meta-cerebration &, &, &

Which it did a little—affect the blood flow to his penis—but not so much to be noticeable, and yet the woman must have noticed because she climbed back onto the bed, the candle left behind on the trunk, its flame wavering, casting now what appeared to the man in his heightened state of nearly unendurable anxiety to be ghastly and lurid shadows around the room, and the woman laid herself between his legs (a position he felt sure was—on some level, conscious or not—a shame-based reaction to his horribly frustrated and desperate and culturally conditioned male gaze that he had just cast upon her, in which gaze she no doubt could perceive the *entirety* of *civilization's* misogynistic, judgmental, damning and hating gaze, the same gaze—he was sure she was sure, given all her research—the same and final gaze that Rebecca Nurse must have witnessed before the gallows' floor flew up past and forever above eye-level; the gaze that Joan of Arc saw through flames, the burning eyes of a crowd that wanted to kill the thing they hated: a woman, he was sure she was sure) and took his penis into her mouth and her mouth felt warm and wet and slow and deep and then, cultural notions of constructed gender identity be damned, his erection began to regain its girth, and the man felt a kind of slow ease of thought that allowed him to think past civilization's long list of misogynistic crimes and to gently focus on his love feelings for this woman, and in this way he began to consider that her breasts were womanly breasts and that they were natural, and in that way, yes, they were in some fashion like a cow's, but only in a fashion that was natural and universally intended and life-sustaining and earth-motherish.

He loved the woman because she was a woman—whatever that meant—the man now understood. She was elemental and erotic and natural and sexy and nurturing and hot. Her wide, natural ass was sexy too, and then the man discovered that there was something intensely arousing about all this *thought*, thinking about loving a woman in all her earthy, fecund womanhood, and, though he was relaxed and contemplative, he could feel his penis straightening and hardening as she worked it in her mouth, aware of his arousal as a response to her natural bodily nature, and all at once the man felt like he was going to climax from thinking of the woman and her natural way—and, dear lord, for what he was about to do next, the man truly hated himself, but nonetheless there was nothing else for it. In order to forestall his sexual climax, he had to concentrate on the erectile-blood-flow-inhibiting long list of civilization's misogynistic crimes—systematic rape in wartime: little girls and teenage girls and young women and middle-aged women and old women pulled out into village squares to be held down, blurry under a dark huddle of soldiers; female genital mutilation: clitorectomies done on women *by* women in Africa and the Middle East (Walker, Steinem, 1989, 1983) as well as Type I FGN taking place *domestically*, in the United States, in fact, right here in New York (Farnes and Hubbard, 1980); the stoning of a Yezidi Kurdish girl for falling in love with a Muslim boy, tricked by her own family into coming out of hiding, and once home, dragged out into the village square, while a thousand men (according to a Jebar news source) stripped her, kicked her, taunted her, publicly inspected her hymen, and then smashed stones onto her head, some of the participants filming the event on cell phones so that web viewers all over the world could see the girl with the smashed face now obscured by blood and brain matter still breathing while she died and the crowd cheering, etc., etc., etc.

But there were complicated implications to this psychic trickery, namely that he now felt complicit in the global patriarchal system of misogyny and sexual objectification that he had so often, publicly and privately, railed against. And he felt stomach-cinching guilt and anger for feeling that he should have to hold back his naturally-occurring-in-the-act-of-love-making-orgasm due to the cultural dictate that said that, as a man, he was supposed to be able to hold off and continue to sexually gratify his partner's vagina with his "rock-hard cock," pulverizing her quivering "pussy" until she came with the bed-quaking ferocity of a seizure victim, then, and only then, allowing his own naturally occurring orgasm to issue forth grandly while holding lovingly and yet masculinely his freshly spent partner as she panted and whimpered and wept and tried to regain her sense of time, space, and dimension.

And thus, in order to achieve the culturally expected—nay, *mandated*—masculine status of "fuck machine" that he had been conditioned to believe he should aspire to, he was guilty of participating in the same cultural conditioning he had abjured for its bringing to his mind the word "teats," the same conditioning he'd moments ago congratulated himself for rejecting, such rejection allowing him to discover his true and natural love feeling for the woman's natural and life-sustaining breasts. And so the man grew ever more depressed as he tried to think quickly and get himself out of this corner and readjust his mind's focus back to the woman who owned these natural breasts. But then words like "voluptuous" and "bodacious" came to him and again he felt his sphincter tighten and testicles make ready to discharge their load, and the man knew it was culturally expected of him to hold back the on-coming orgasm, and all at once he felt exhausted with sex, depleted with the demands of being a man for this woman even during sex, and he felt even more exhausted when he considered that the very good thing he had wanted to be for the woman was itself culturally conditioned. For what did he mean when he thought that he wanted to be a man for her? What was a man? Nothing at all, he knew, let's face it, but a culturally conditioned set of gender expectations and constructions that at once made him feel good and honest, but also despicable and deceiving and deceived.

And so, despairing of knowing himself, he wanted to know the woman. He reached down and touched her face, letting his hand send a message that he wanted her to come up from between his thin, hairless legs to be face-to-face with him on their bed.

V. NOW AND YOU KNOW YOU MUST

Another thing that can kill a mood and increase one's self-consciousness (not that anyone but the woman could have the final say in how she felt about how the culture made her feel, Barbara had helped her recognize and work to accept that fact) and make one hate even more deeply one's own body is any break from the complete confidence you have that your partner has anything but totally, utterly aroused sexual thoughts and feelings about you when you're having sex, even if you're not exactly having sex yet, but are in fact making ready a candle that will initiate the both of you to a whole new experience of sex together; trying to believe all that when a man is doing a Brandoesque performance is difficult enough, but when you look up from bending naked and see your partner looking at you as though he were trying to decide if he should still eat a piece of pizza that fell on the floor, then you have a mighty battle ahead of you indeed. And the woman knew this.

Standing before his eyes, under his gaze, the woman knew it all. Knew the way the long line of days and years would unspool with this man, with all men, truth be told. The breasts were, if she were being now very, very honest with herself, not the whole problem. She'd have the surgery, she knew it now, but that would change nothing. The bed would still be here when she returned from the hospital, the sofa, the bookcase, the trunk, the candle, and the man. The only way she'd make it through the next day was to say goodbye to her body the way she had planned. But now she knew, and in knowing she would never again ever. . . .

And so, under his gaze, his terrified eyes seeing her eyes noticing him gazing at her, she needed to reduce this moment to something less conscious, he being aware of her awareness of his awareness, and all that. For if she stayed standing, leaving him alone on the bed, registering her hurt and outrage at what they both knew had just happened, they'd have to talk; and she knew the man would try to explain himself, would try to "assuage her feelings," which sincere albeit somewhat selfish effort would, in fact, be mood-murdering. And so because this was not about him anymore, not about *them* even—but rather about what she needed to do now for herself, in this last time with her body, her body as it was now and never would be again—because she needed to do this for herself, she smiled to reassure the man that she was still ready for him, smiled as she crawled up between his legs, smiled—though, had he spoken one word, she knew she would have had to ask him to please be quiet, to please shut up, to please, please, please, please, please, please. . . .

VI. &, &, &, &, &, &, ...

And as she was coming up, she did not reach for the candle
but instead smiled at him from down there, the smile he
had fallen deeply in love with once, which he remembered
had occurred at a restaurant over a paper-covered table
on their third date. And the smile was, like his love for
her, not one that most people would call perfect. It wasn't
winning or seductive or tempting or sweet. It was shy. It
involved the shy muscles in and around the mouth. A
semi-smile. A smile too conscious of itself. One side of
her face pulled back just a bit more than the other, in a
way that reminded him of a stroke victim, but her crooked
smile now was precisely the smile that he had noticed at
the restaurant and he could not believe he had not noticed it before their third date. And when the woman
put herself on top of him, and slid onto what was now his
thoroughly erect penis, something inside him that was not
his lungs exhaled, and he shuddered and simultaneously
sighed and was overcome with the need to push as much
of himself inside her as could reach. What a fellow on his
college crew team used to call being "balls deep." A term
he had despised, but now felt a strange new understanding of and identification with. Which, of course, caused
the man to worry he was guilty of enacting an even more
complicated set of gender constructions and alliances. But
he was still thinking about that sigh, which contempla-
tion crowded out, for the moment, his gender guilt and
attendant anxiety and depression. He thought it was an
emotional response he was having, one connected to his
love feelings for the woman. The feeling was comforting
and sleeplike, but not unconscious. In fact, he felt utterly
conscious, aware of many things at once. But for the first
time in a long time, these awarenesses did not ignite his

guilt and anxiety and attendant depression. Nor did they affect his erection.

When she had gotten comfortable on him, she lowered her face to his and did not affect a fake kind of passionate kiss but simply touched her tongue to his lips, the man overwhelmed by a fullness in his soul, his eyes burning, and he thought about how just moments earlier there had been a flash of culturally conditioned judgment that made him question his "true" feelings for this woman and that the feelings of judgment were about her breasts, the very things he wanted her not to loathe due to what he considered to be their shared curse of cultural conditioning, and which breasts he could now feel brushing against his own breasts—or, more preferably to his gender-constructed and culturally conditioned way of thinking: pectoral muscles.

He thought about the new feeling of *not* caring about the shape of her breasts, and the erotic understanding of how they were beautiful in a way that was new to his understanding, they were natural and yes, okay, fine, *cowlike* in their biological function, and how humans and animals weren't different after all, and how that was not something he needed to be scared of, but erotically aroused by, erotic like eros, the life force, and which realization could send a mega-charge of erotic electrical current through his penis, which penis was now being rubbed by the insides of her vagina, and her wetness made him want to hold her head and kiss her more like a man would kiss a woman he loved, which thought had a double effect of making him, now in his comfortable, erotically charged state, laugh at the when-you-came-right-down-to-it flimsy culturally implanted picture of how a man should romantically kiss a woman, and how he wanted her to feel kissed in the way a woman in a romantic movie would feel, and yet he also felt that regardless of filmic representations of kisses, he actually really *did* want to kiss her just like that and while thinking these thoughts, he acted on instinct (not questioning for the moment that problematic term) and went ahead and did it, moved her head gently and kissed her, all the while feeling that his own breast did not even give milk and that one day, if genetics could be predicted from memories at the beach with his father and grandfather, that one day his breasts would look not only not as nice as they did now due to regular visits to the gym, but that his breasts would look like hers, like a woman's breasts, as did his father's and grandfather's, doughy flat sacks that would hang conically when he bent to hammer into the sand the female end of the cone that would receive the male end of the beach umbrella, and that his male breasts would dangle and conically hang while he hammered and jiggled the beach umbrella, in plaid shorts with black stockings in sandals.

He would be on that future beach with this woman whose breasts he years before had had a weirdness about, but who now—in his female-breast-stage—would love him as he loved her ultimately, a generous love, and pushing within her he felt the deep-sigh and comfort feeling again, and he released hard inside the woman, arching his feet and curling his nine toes and almost could not stand the sensation along with the attendant idea that his sperm might make a baby inside her this very night and how natural and animallike that would be, foals and all that. And the man hoped the woman did become pregnant because, though he hadn't yet told her, she was the one woman in his life whom he now would seriously consider marrying. (In the future, of course, after they had talked through all the implications of participating in and thus validating socially constructed bourgeois notions of marriage.) Yes, she was the woman he could seriously consider one day marrying. He knew this now.

VII. Reductio ad Recessus

And after the sex, as they lay in each other's arms, he tried to tell her what he thought about her breasts, tried to "share" his thoughts and feeling with the woman. But first he needed to qualify his comments and explain that he was in no way trying to "save" her or "rescue" her from her broken situation, but that Gramsci be damned, he and she, he now understood clearly, were both of animal stock. No better than rutting barnyard creatures. He told her that her breasts were like a cow's teats. He tried to communicate some of the beauty and awe of this realization, especially as it had bearing on his love feelings for her, while also trying to communicate some of the complications of what he felt regarding the similarities between her breasts and a cow's teats. He tried to explain the shared cultural conditioning and possibly soon-to-be-shared mammaric conicallity. And he held her, and she did not react the way he thought she would to hearing his words, did not seem to be filled with the same cathartic emotion he had just experienced. She didn't seem to grasp the enormous significance of how he had felt and now did feel, how he had "worked through" his confusion, how he had "broken through" certain barriers—if only for the moment—of the culture's soul-crippling conditioning. He recalled something she mentioned once while reading from a book she kept on her bedside table: What you don't work through for yourself, you will act out in your relationships (Bradshaw, 1992). He felt he now had a glimmer of what it meant to "work through" something. He nearly understood. And he would share this shared therapeutic sensibility with her. He was nearly giddy realizing that he might have, to some extent and properly understood, "broken through."

But the woman seemed stiff in his arms. And it was her stiffness that convinced him he should hold in abeyance for the moment the whole marriage-realization-break-through thing. Just for now. But he was still euphoric lying with her, and he wanted to communicate some of that euphoria to her, wanted to communicate clearly (as clearly as possible given the built-in limitations of language) how he felt about her, which feelings were to his mind loving feelings. There was so much he wanted to bring to her in that moment. Their shared struggle. The curse of the culture. The possibility of marriage. Of children. The man wanted the woman to understand that though she would perhaps always be broken, he would be broken with her. Possibly for the rest of their lives—if, of course, they talked and shared and understood all of the ramifications of what "the rest of their lives" actually meant.

The woman responded by repeating her belief that it was important that she be honest with the man, telling him that she yet again had not had an orgasm, but that she had still felt incredibly close to him, closer than she had ever felt to him—or anyone—before, and that she felt, despite what the culture would have one believe, that, sometimes, at least, it really is different for a woman, and that, despite not reaching orgasm, she was glad that he had. And the man restated how he felt about her breasts, the complicated admiration and love feelings, and he added that he wanted her to know something: that her breasts were beautiful and exactly as nature intended, and that she should not change them or alter them to suit anybody but herself. He swallowed hard, as he knew all clichéd culturally conditioned men in his position would, and tried to tell the woman, tried to tell the woman, tried to tell the woman, tried to tell. His eye twitched. Hers were closed. And the man held the woman and the woman held the man and the bed was to both of them a place to rest for the moment.

Everlovin'

"Well, look who it is. How did you find us? Seems like nobody knows we're here or even cares. Here, hey. So how did you manage to . . . ? Few were able. Most of them are gone, you know. If you came back to find them. The others are gone too. It's just us now—me and Kenny—we're sort of like clean-up men. The others don't want to look at it. Can't blame them. I'm not doing too well, either. Kenny's in charge. The whole thing makes me a little so I can't stop too long or sleep—just the thoughts, you know, keep coming in. Everyday something. Not like you're gonna forget. Jesus Christ, it was so. . . . I mean, I was so—terrified's not the right word but yeah, the whole time. Still feel terrified, like it's *of* me now, you know. Scared the cock out of me, I'll tell you."

"Did you—?"

"Yeah, sure, I was there. I mean, not there-there. I was hiding like everyone else. You couldn't not. They were just everywhere all of a sudden, and we weren't ready. Came down on us like a cloudburst. Everyone running for cover. Lost a couple of mine that first hour. Scared the cock out of me."

"Did you say . . . ? Scared the what out of you?"

"Sure, I was scared. No shame in admitting that. We all were. I mean, where do these guys learn their tactics? I mean, that's kitchenware, right? I'm not crazy here, am I? That's stuff you use in a kitchen. But, oh Christ, what they did with it. And most of those were children. *With stuff we use in our kitchens.* I'm getting the jeebies again. You want another hit of this? Here, hey. Go on, there's tons left. They didn't touch this stuff. Nah, it's like they came to take one thing only. And I guess they did. I mean, you can tell from the smell right? Blind person'd know something happened here. Scared the cock out of me."

"You say 'cock,' right? You're saying the word 'cock'?"

"Terrified. It's true. Completely terrified. You don't know fear like that. This isn't like being-scared fear, this is faith-molesting fear. Got it? This kind of fear I'm talking about contaminates you, works on your cells, not just your nerves."

"Okay, got it, but—just, please, for me, for a second: 'cock,' right? Was it 'cock'? The word was 'cock'? Your cock? Someone's . . . ? Whose cock are we—?"

"Sure, we were all cut faithless that day. I mean, Kenny was there. He had to watch when they did it to his little girl. Held her down on a table and made him watch for trying to charge one of them. Touched the tip of a steak knife blade to his eye and said they'd carve it out if he closed it. That's why Kenny's the way he is now. Was Kenny the one that first told it was kitchenware. You don't need a very big piece of kitchenware to take what they came here to take. Except, even Kenny, as zipped-off and crazy as he is right now—and let me tell you, he's zipped-off—even Kenny's afraid to touch the jar. Afraid to take it down from that shelf. He'll clean everything else. Even the table. You just can't look at that jar. Scares the everlovin' cock out of you."

"It is, I mean, it is . . . it is 'cock,' right? I got that straight. You're saying cock? You're talking about cock, right? Because this is not something of a phrase I've ever heard before."

"Terrifying. The table's out back. Kenny lugged it out there to hose it down. He's been hosing it down for two days now. Says he can still see the stains. Looks clean to me but there it is. That's the contamination I'm talking about. We were all contaminated that day. I mean, let me tell you: we were scared *crotchless*."

"You know what? Clarification's all I'm asking for. So, may I . . . please, for the love of, is it, can we, all I'm, did you, can we just go back for a minute? Can I just—did you say . . . ?"

"Here, hey."

"I don't want that shit. That's why all this happened and you know it. So keep your fucking 'Here, hey.' What I want is I'm trying to understand something is all I'm saying is what I want. So, now, tell me: Did you, I mean, was it, did you, it was, wasn't it? That, that word you used?"

"Ask Kenny."

"Who the fuck is Kenny? What are we talking about here? I don't understand what we're talking about."

"I know, it's beyond words, isn't it? I mean, your little girl . . . well . . . your little girl, too."

"No. No. No. No. No. No. Now. Now. Now. Now. Now. Now. It is. I mean. You say. It is, I mean, it is cock, right? Just tell me that. I only want to understand that much. Beyond cock, I'm not ready to go yet."

"You wanna understand? Just turn around and look up. The shelf there. But you better prepare yourself first. Here, hey. Here, hey. Good. There you go: nice and deep. Now, when you're ready, slowly turn around and look up. There you go. Whoa, hey, easy. Simmer down. Here, hey. Okay, so now you see? You see now? Better take it in, fella. You come back here and you dare ask me about. . . . There's no answer for that. Answers were not given. Answers will not be given. You understand as much as any of us understands—and more than most could even give a hoot."

The Subjunctive Mood

(1) A condition contrary to fact; (2) an expression of a wish; (3) a command or request: e.g., Suppose, in your attempt to be as humorous as a new friend of yours—a new colleague in the English department, a grammar teacher who'd somehow never heard of crickets and silence, a lovely new friend whose natural ease with humor genuinely delights you more sometimes than even sex with this new friend, an activity that you and your humorous new friend have recently taken up as merrily as a couple might begin tennis lessons—you try every new joke that comes to mind in an attempt to amuse that humorous friend. You observe that often, while on the phone with her, after your aforementioned attempts at humor, there is often silence. Only the forlorn crackle of static. So at some point in that dearth of response you utter a follow-up joke. The most obvious image that comes to mind in that desperate moment is some memory of . . . what? A television show? A cartoon, perhaps? *The Flintstones*, maybe? Some episode of *The Flintstones* in which Fred tries his hand at stand-up: he poised awkwardly, so unboisterously Fred-like, at a prehistorically chrono-appropriate microphone: a seashell, perhaps, some natural pre-Edisonian echo chamber, some organic vessel that augments his voice for all to hear in the auditorium of the Royal Order of Water Buffalos, the Grand Poobah in

his grand fez sitting at first upright, attentive, alert, like a little boy, his bare toes wiggling, eager for the serotonin-rich cascade of laughter that cures all ills, then a cutaway back to Fred alone, silent on stage, sweating, fingering his increasingly snug loincloth collar, clearing his throat; he tosses out a joke, some Youngmanesque groaner, and we cut back to the Grand Poobah, now slouching back in his prehistoric stone chair, not smiling, a frown of impatience knotting his brow, his Fez looking, judging by his expression, like a two-ton lampshade. But then Fred rallies; he launches into the Big Joke, the killer that he rehearsed in front of Wilma ad infinitum at the dinner table until we get a cutaway to Wilma's face, the blank face of a zombie, her neck stalk-stiff, her eyes little spirals spinning like a child's toy, the same joke he worked out over and over again with Barney while at work at the quarry, his boss, Mr. Slate, observing from his office window, peering every few seconds at his stone-age watch (a tiny sundial sprouting a small stone cut at a right angle), Mr. Slate tsk-tsking, his face turning red until smoke comes out of his ears and he yells, "Flintstooooooooooone, cut out the jokes and get back to work!" Back onstage, Fred launches into that well-oiled killer joke, his setup smooth, natural, all the kinks worked out from myriad practice runs, practice making both him and us think it the perfect delivery; we love Fred, we learn how to be human from Fred, we learn to laugh at ourselves, at our foibles and failures, at our shortcomings and at our always-yearning human heart, a heart unsatisfied with quarry work, a heart always asking, Is that all there is to this life?: Fred-as-Christ, Fred-as-Poohbear, Fred-as-Everyman, Fred, our savior. We don't so much laugh at his joke as much as we enter Fred's consciousness of his telling the joke, the nimble shifts in tone and vocal range that are necessary for accomplishing this soon-to-be-side-splitter; we unconsciously mouth the words, we frown when Fred frowns for effect, gesture lightly as Fred gestures, we are now one with Fred, Fred-as-all-of-us, we tapping into the very Fredness we all carry inside us like some atavistic gene. And finally, when the punch line is in view, we get ourselves ready to be adored; we know we deserve this; we've felt along with Fred every neural stimulation that went into telling this joke; we imagine the warm pats on the back at the water cooler, the reverential handshake Barney will give us backstage, the raise in salary that Mr. Slate will give us for fear that we will quit the quarry and seek stardom on the comedy nightclub circuit, polishing our act until the one day (quite soon, no doubt) that we are asked to be a guest on *The Tonight Show* (the other guest that evening being the sexy Ann-Margrock), but we know, like the archer who is not the archer but the arrow, that we must forget all that ego-business and stay focused on the joke; we are not merely the deliverer of this joke, we are the joke, the narrator and the narrative, speaker and poem, painter and paint, the dancer and the dance—we are, in short, humor itself. And so, like a diver whose toes let go the stippled, abrasive edge of the diving board, we too let go of all control and free-fall into that punch line, splashing into that blue mirror, below whose unknowable surface we all must plunge if we are ever to achieve anything of worth on this planet. And down below—our bodies floating prenatally, the soon-to-be-unleashed applause still muffled overhead—we can't help but smile, alone down there in the egoless womb, we smile, not so much at the funniness of the joke, but at the fact of the funniness, the fact that we've brought funniness into the world for all to share, the ultimate act of generosity, one mere human giving something selflessly to another. We allow ourselves to feel good for the first time in months—we weren't sure we'd even remembered how.

And then, when we have done all we can, we finally allow the prodigal ego back to greet its just reward. And, in our complete oneness with Fred, we feel exactly as Fred feels, we experience the same states of emotion, even the same trauma that blossoms like a poison flower when, the camera still panned excruciatingly on Fred, no view yet provided of the audience, the only sound emanating from the vast Royal Order of Water Buffalo auditorium is not laughter, but the itchy, dry, deathlike sound of crickets.

We have been imprinted with that sound. And years later, far away from that TV and that warm home, we talk on the phone to our new friend and try our own killer, and when that fails, both Fred's and, by cathartic extension, our own trauma is reactivated, and we reach for whatever we can to salvage our joke, our self-respect, our human worth; we say, "I think I hear the sound of crickets."

The joke gets a laugh. We live to see another day. But then, a couple of days after, in another part of the metropolis, some Iowan poet upon a stage finds the same words for his discomfort, finds the need to share those words with an audience of his own, and, in the universe's cosmic-comic twist, in that very audience is seated our new friend, the one who laughed at our joke, but who, instead of smiling along with the others, frowns like the Grand Poobah, and thinks: crickets, crickets, crickets. When she calls you to tell you she thought you had made up the joke, was disappointed that you had led her to believe you had, you accuse her of lying, of always knowing about crickets and silence. This exchange is followed by more silence.

Q: What would you do if you were me? Plead your case, say it was entirely your own original joke, argue that you must be tapped into some cosmic-comic funniness that all Iowan poets and prehistoric men understand? Or say, "OK, yes, I did hear the joke elsewhere. Who hasn't? How could you have not? Perhaps it was at camp, or on some TV show, I can't recall. But I'm sorry. I wanted to tell you sooner, but you seemed so amused; everything was perfect; and weren't we happy? Didn't you like me just a little bit more? Find my lazy eye just a little less disconcerting? Feel comfortable having merry new sex because I too am funny and attractive? Like you. And don't you like me more than the me whom I don't let you see? Can't I be forgiven for trying to stave off the inevitable? What would you do? If you were me?

Unheimliche

But it's not exactly like that either—at least not entirely—not exactly like what you said I just said. But, okay, fine, I could go that far. I could. Since you're pressing me on what was meant to be a toss-off comment about living abroad, about being a woman living abroad with strangers in a home that's not my home, that's not even a home at all. But since living with strangers in a hostel seems—according to your definition—to require a certain level of self-disclosure, a level of self-disclosure that you claim Americans don't possess, then, fine, I will try to explain. Try to make you understand. I guess what all I'm saying is that, regardless of your assertion of the quote inherent contradiction in my logic, it does, indeed, sort of *feel* that way. Okay? You following me? It's a *feeling*. I guess I'll just put it like that—since you want to nail me down on this point—it's about the strangeness of feeling at home, at home anywhere, not just *here* or *there*—those political binaries you so ardently invoke—but rather the *strangeness* of feeling *at home*, a feeling of *anti-at-homeness*, what I believe you all here call *das Unheimliche*. So, no, I can't go so far as to say it's about actually feeling *at home*, rather it was about *feeling* like *being* at home, what *being home* would feel like, but also at the same time feeling a contrapuntal feeling such as *This isn't at all what a home should be*, feeling like feeling homey feels frightening, feels wrong, like feeling at home is a bad thing, like a homesickness, a nausea. Something. However, the idea of an actual home, of a space and place constructed from the elements of home—i.e., hard roof, front porch, a cold, damp cellar, a backyard burial ground for our dead—is a good thing. Brings up good feelings. Good home vs. Bad home. But because this place we are presently in isn't my real home, but a home I live in now away from home, an away-from-home home that I share with other people and yet still is a home that has formed some impression on me, some emotional response that I am able to articulate only barely to you, to you and your prodding, and because you say that this is just quote romantic American female bullshit unquote, all I can say is I'm sorry but it feels that way to me, okay? So when I say that I dream about being home and that this hostel is starting to feel like my home, I do not mean my actual home, my homeland, my *Über Alles*, I mean it feels like I'm at *a* home—i.e., I see walls, I hear voices, I smell bodies, that suffocating smell of sleeping bodies wafting over these bunks—but I know it's not my real home, okay? So, no, I'm not trying to export to your great nation whatever the hell you called any quote unquote American Domestic Walmart Policy. I'm just trying to describe how I feel here in this home that's not my home. Surely, you, an architectural student, a *German* architectural student, can understand something about that. And, no, it has nothing to do with my dream-home that I made the unfortunate mistake of telling you about this morning, and that you now want me to explain to your satisfaction, because, as I've already stated, that dream-home was not even necessarily this hostel; it was just a place that felt and kind of looked like this hostel, a place where we all lived but didn't really live. See, that's why explaining this is hard, because it wasn't exactly like that. Not exactly. We lived here, but I also lived here alone sometimes. Like, as in I didn't feel the presence of others while those others surrounded me. And it was precisely the living-there-alone-but-with-other-people feeling that the dream was all about. In a certain way. Okay, listen, I got it, here's what it is: that the house is my house, but it isn't my house at home, where I used to live, and where you keep referring to as *There*. In this dream, I am living in a house, but nothing ever happens. I mean, there's no story to my dream, no narrative, no plot. Although maybe sometimes something happens, like something sort of scary happens, sometimes, maybe. But in this house it's never the type of scary like in a nightmare-scary. This is not a nightmare. More often it's something quotidian, like there's no food in the fridge, but then the sight of the empty fridge, the smell of its vacant plastic walls sort of freaks me out, I guess a little bit it scares me, like how I was freaking out after we smoked that guy's hash last week, and but then for some reason my mother is here, and she tells me that I'm duty-bound as a guest of this hostel to resolve this situation, that I'm to leave earlier for school that day, and that she will give me money to go to the store and get the food that the fridge so sadly lacks, but the thought of me (a me who, weirdly, in this dream, is my exact age today, a girl of twenty-five; but I *feel* like I'm around the age of nine or ten) going to the store alone before school for some reason scares the shit out of me, maybe it's the language thing, maybe it's the foreign geography, I don't know, but so I'm looking twenty-five but feeling nine or ten, wearing a pink bookbag, shuffling down the street in my little pink sneakers that I used to love, I'm shuffling with my head hung low, scraping along, mumbling angry mumbles to myself about why there's no food in the fridge and why my mother has let our domestic affairs fall to such a reprehensible level, but really I'm not angry at her, I'm just starting to get angry in general because I hate to feel scared, and yet I feel utterly scared that I'm going to get lost going so far from home, or that something scary will happen to me on the way to the store or to school, even something like getting in trouble for being late to school because I was too scared and stupid to find my way home from the store, a store that all the other kids know how to get to, but a store that to me seems light years away from everything that feels good and safe in my life, like my house at home, like my mother, like my father's grave in our old backyard in the house we used to live in, the burial site marked by a small stone my mother rolled out there, a stone that, on a warm autumn day, we both painted blue and purple and yellow flowers upon, but then all of a sudden, my backyard is still my backyard, but now when I turn around the house that isn't my home doesn't look like this hostel anymore but looks like my old best-friend Jenny's house, but Jenny's house isn't her home, it's a shopping mall—is, in fact, the shopping mall I used to hang out at near my old house back home, and Jenny lives in the shopping mall now, but they have stores they didn't have when I used to hang out there, stores with names like Skechers and Quiksilver, Journeys, and Juicy Couture, Hot Topic, and I'm trying to ask Jenny if I can just take stuff for free, and then I remember the food I was supposed to pick up before school, and then I touch my pocket, but my mother's money is gone, but then I immediately forget all of that because when I look up, Jenny is still Jenny but now looks just like the girl I secretly used to have a crush on in my freshman year of high school (a field hockey player with the strongest calves you've ever seen), and who, five years later, ended up at a party at my college one weekend and whom I kissed all night in my bed and took to the cafeteria the next morning where I got her in for free with my meal pass, and she ate seven pancakes, and no one ever knew—except, I think, her brother, who actually attended my college, and who, I think, suspected something because later that semester at another party, outside the door to the bathroom, he told me that he wanted to fuck me, actually used that very word, leaned against the wall and used that very word, and so I told him to come into the bathroom with me, and we both peed, and then I took my hand and shook off his last drops, but nothing happened to him down there, and he got all weird and contemplative and looked away and said he thought it was because I was a dyke, a dyke who slept with his dyke sister, and, you know, I don't even like girls all that much anymore, and not because I am, as you called me yesterday, a quote American prude, but because I currently happen to be more into guys than girls right now—but so anyway: so this girl, the one with the calves, it turns out she doesn't live at the mall that is Jenny's house, she lives here in Germany, is in fact in the army stationed in Germany, and she sends me pictures and writes e-mails about her small cottage in Andernach, a cottage that she shares with some other people who aren't soldiers but who are students, German students, who despite being dream-construed as students, actually look just like the soldiers in Iraq—green T-shirts and baggy pants, cigarettes and pointing fingers, and then all of a sudden it's that other house where she lives, my German dream-house (that term that was so off-pissing to you earlier), only yet now she doesn't live there, I do, and it's not in Andernach anymore, it's here, in Hamburg, but it doesn't feel like here, it feels like the house I grew up in, the house that is my home, and my mother is always in rooms other than those that I'm in, and I can hear her talking and her voice is quiet and old, and she carries a shovel and even though she never wears T-shirts, she's wearing my father's old sweat-stained T-shirt with the droopy v-neck collar, and she looks older than I've ever seen her, and I get scared again, but not like a nightmare-scared, but like something harder to describe, something like the empty-fridge feeling, something almost uncanny, something unhomely, but this feeling only lasts a little while, and then I force myself to wake up—an ability I possess that, despite your claiming it to be bullshit, has actually been the very thing that has saved me so many times from choking on the smell of all these bodies.

Postcard

Postmark: 31 October 2001

Here's the way it looks now, since I know you'd want to know, since you're the reason I moved here, since it was you who loved cities and tall buildings and myriad faces, and since it was you who said, Go to Big Apple, get that degree; but don't forget to write. I didn't forget. I sent something off to you once. And that too was a postcard. Just before you went into the hospital for good, remember? It was a picture of those two big towers, the ones we had stood atop, you pointing your shaking finger north to Boston, saying I think I see the Prudential. All around us was sky. You told me how you took Mom to its top to cure her fear of heights.

Let me tell you how it looks now. Where I'm standing, on Bleecker and MacDougal, you'd never know by merely looking (though if you closed your eyes and inhaled, you'd know something had happened here). But today there is no sign of it anywhere, no rubble, no trucks, no bucket brigades, none of that white dust. I can't even spot a Xeroxed flier. Just tables and chairs—a bit emptier than usual, but out and open for business, as everyone keeps repeating. There are some little kids in costumes—though rarely without an adult hand hovering nearby. And seeing them made me think of you, the time you were here last, in '98, when you came to visit before I graduated. We walked past the apartment in the Village where your brother had lived back in the 40s. It took you a while to remember its location. You said it was because the city was different then. How changed it all seemed to you now.

We sat here at this café. We waited twenty minutes for a table; today I'm the only customer. We sat and drank coffee as black as your eyes, and though your memory was starting to go in that awful way it would go, you told me stories, you loved stories, you had hundreds of stories, all of them now seeming to tie into each other, digressing into other narratives with similar points of ingress. (I guess I'm guilty of that too. All I seem to do these days is babble.) You repeated your Prudential story about Mom and her fear of towers, and I pretended it was the first time I'd heard it; and that story lead to another story concerning the first time we had stepped atop those two towers, a year before, when we looked out across this island, directed our eyes north through the clouds, north to Boston, back to where the others had boarded those planes, planes bound for a heaven that would contain both them and you. (Am I romanticizing it? I need a place to remember you, is all.) And that's when you suggested we go there again, remember? We waved the waiter over and you spoke Italian to him, and although I couldn't fully understand what you were saying, I saw him laugh, his mustached mouth spreading east and west. You looked at me then, your eyes glinting, as if proving to me that you could still make contact with this world. We paid Carlo in cash, and I dropped an extra dollar. And you and I set off for the tip of Manhattan. As we walked down Church Street, I recited from memory Whitman's "Give Me the Splendid Silent Sun," and although you couldn't fully understand what I was saying, you smiled when I finished and said, "Good boy, well done, you have an excellent memory." And you reached out and shook my hand like a man trying to hold on tight to something. Then you were silent for a while, looking fearlessly ahead. We were both silent for a while, just the two of us, walking south, the white chasms of lower New York like a crater we would never find our way out of.

Late Thaw

Who thinks these things as you eat a peanut butter sandwich and your wife is lacing up her Nikes in the kitchen
and warning you to go slow with the bread and asking you
to stay put because she has a job for you, in about one
second you are going to hold her left ankle and lift it incrementally as she lets unstiffen her hamstring and
breathes deeply and bunches her brow and puts all her
weight in your hands and says she's going to take advantage
of her day off and greater advantage still of the weather
because no one's going to be running in the park on a day
like this, overcast and cold and two days before Thanks-
giving, no strollers, no bikes, and won't she be thus utterly
allowed to give herself over to it, let herself go, run without thought as she did as a girl on the beaches of Cape
Cod, that place she took you to after only two months of
dating to meet her family because she said without any
sentimentality at all because that is not her style, just said
it like she might be giving someone the time, that she
wants you to meet her father before he dies, because he's
dying, she told you and then never mentioned it again;
and she drives you in another November from New York
to Massachusetts in her old white Subaru with no working
heat and you play the only cassette tape she has in the car
which is the B-52s Cosmic Thing and you thrill at the

slate-gray planks of water miles it seems below you as you cross the Sagamore Bridge and then continue down old Route 6 past houses with unpainted clapboards and scrub brush and white pine until she takes some turns and then more and then swings the Subaru into a driveway made of beach sand, and parks in front of an open, empty garage but not inside the garage and a big, rusty-blond dog comes ambling out of the house and although strange dogs scare you you nonetheless put your hand out for sniff-inspection and your soon-to-be-though-you-don't-know-it-yet wife drops to her knees and lets go her backpack and puts her mittened hands out and says, Rexford, come here, Rexford, and a woman with short, neatly combed white hair comes onto the porch wearing a faded denim shirt over a dark turtleneck, and says to you, Well, hello there, and to your girlfriend says, If you want to park in the garage that's fine because Roberta's left for the day, and you shake hands with the white-haired woman who tells you to call her Ellen, and then around your legs and into the house runs the dog before you even make it to the steps, and inside on a couch under a patch quilt and comforter is a man with no hair and breathtakingly thin and his name is Mike and Mike doesn't stand to shake hands but does nonetheless offer you his hand to shake, and his hand feels dry and cool and as hollow as a bird, but is bumpy with calluses, and later after dinner when your future wife and her mother are washing dishes he says to you something that could, if you allowed it to, sound to your graduate-school ears like something worthy of critical ridicule, but that, later upon reflection, under the circumstances sounds to you not merely nonsentimental but utterly heroic, life-affirming, real, is delivered, in fact, as if he were just giving someone the time, he says—My daughter likes you, and I may not get to see her get mar-

ried but she likes you and so what the hell, I'll say it to
you. If you should end up with her please take good care
of her, I'm supposed to say that, right, well, you probably
already picked on this, but she's a tough girl, believe me
I know, she won't always let you know what she's thinking
and she'll keep you out of her life sometimes even when
you don't understand why she would feel she couldn't trust
someone who loves her as much as you do. Believe me I
know, take it from me, he says, she's a tough one. But she's
an honest girl. Once saw her from a doorway when she
never knew I was watching stand on her bare toes trying
to reach a book off a shelf and knock over one of them
boats-in-a-bottle that my father had made me; he had
dozens of those pieces of shit. Anyway, it hit the side of
the dresser and scattered in shards around her bare feet,
and I stepped back quick knowing she'd hate that I'd seen
her, but she didn't see me and so I figured I'd better keep
my mouth shut, just crept down the stairs and headed out
to check my lobster traps because I didn't want any trouble
from that girl, nope, learned my lesson early, and listen
to me here: one wrong move, one wagged finger with that
one and she'd be silent for days. Better to keep the peace
than to rail about an old bottle, I figured. But then later
that night, Ellen told me that our girl had been brooding
all day, quiet and slouchy, kinda food fickle, passed up a
Hoodsie cup her mother'd offered her, but then finally
before bed had confided in her mother that she had broken the boat-in-the-bottle that Grampa had given Daddy
and that on her own she'd cleaned up the floor and saved
all the pieces in a brown paper bag, and then she lifted
her bare feet and my wife saw what some of that brooding
had been about and told our daughter to stay put while
she fetched the Mercurochrome, and . . . aw, hell, I got
a million stories about how she has made me proud that

I was saving for someday to tell her like maybe on her wedding day, that's what we're supposed to do, right? Fathers and daughters? But I guess that is the way life finally does go. I'm sure I'm not telling you nothing new, nothing you don't already think about, but it's worth repeating, I think: You better do some things while you are still able because one day you might not have that chance again—and that was all Mike had wanted to say to you, and that night Mike and Ellen let you and their daughter sleep premaritally in her old bedroom, and when, in the dark, her back in your belly, you told her the story that Mike had told you, you felt her face and it was wet and the next morning you woke alone, and downstairs Ellen was sitting with Mike and a woman dressed in white who said her name was Roberta, and Ellen said that their daughter had gone for a run on the beach and that you should pour yourself a cup of coffee in the kitchen, and by the time your cup was full the back door swung open and in with cold air she came, pulling off hat and mittens, and said, God, how good that felt, had the beach all to herself; and two days later day you were back in Brooklyn, and sometimes you would look out the window of your apartment, out onto North 3rd Street, thinking about how he lived long enough to know that she was engaged to be married to you but not long enough to see her get married, and how his voice was hard to hear and he didn't say much over the phone when you called to ask his permission, and okay maybe that was too schmaltzy and maybe you rushed things a bit because of the talk you and Mike had had, but you never cared or believed you made the wrong decision because she was a tough girl and she told the truth and maybe she hid herself away sometimes but she always came back—except from the park, because who thinks these things, that while your wife is lacing up her Nikes and you're eating a sandwich made from the bread you were supposed to use for the stuffing for a turkey that will sit in your freezer frozen for seven months until you finally throw it out because you couldn't until now because it was she who had touched it last, she who had brought it home a week before her run and cleared out the freezer shelf and pushed the frozen bird in, and who thinks these things, that while all this is happening a man who lives a state and a river away and who has driven many times through and has studied the landscape of the same park your wife will jog through that very afternoon will also take advantage of a day when the visibility is low and the chance of many people being in the park slim, and who thinks these things that this man would use nylon rope that could so easily be traced back to a Home Depot in New Jersey and that he would with that nylon rope make your wife to lie cold in the dirt at the bottom of a slope by the side of the path where no one would find her until after midnight, in fact, not a no one but a dog, a dog would find her running shorts first and the rest of her later, and who thinks these things that her legs that you had helped stretch just hours before would be cold to the touch and so would the feet, and who thinks about these things so much, about if her white and purple running sneakers were on or off those feet, and who thinks these things that this man from across the river would feel convinced that he had studied everything as well as he could, thought of all possible outcomes, but that he would never know that the person he had selected had once long ago in a room where you could always smell the sea broken a bottle with a boat in it and that those glass shards, when her father had turned his back, cut their way into her bare feet? And who thinks these things that those small scars that you had touched and traced and kissed might have gleamed for just a moment in the beam

of a searching flashlight? Who think these things, you
wonder, staring out onto North 3rd Street. Who would
think such things? And for how much longer?

Practice Problem

Circles, overlapping circles, circles intersecting with other circles, like the slow closing interstice of moon crossing over soon-to-be-eclipsed sun, circles overlapping with small shaded areas of geometry, not the geometry of Lobachevsky or Gauss or Euclid, but the geometry of Jennifer, the geometry of Jennifer Hampton, small-boned, green-eyed, pale-faced, goth-girl, theatre major at the state college in Salem, Massachusetts, a women's studies minor currently on academic probation, for the fall semester of 1995, for failing *Introduction to Geometry* last spring, a writer of poetry and nude dancer at Shelby's Slink Factory on Route One, where Jennifer sticks out her pierced tongue and makes contact with her pierced nipple raised by hand up to her black-lipsticked mouth, Jennifer, Jennifer Hampton, the geometry thereof, and those circles, overlapping circles, circles like her silver sunglasses, the ones she wears day and night, indoors and out; circles like her many pills, the ones that deter pregnancy and manic depression, social anxiety disorder and panic attacks, OCD, ADHD, and PTSD; circles like the Sunbeam clock above the dish-filled sink, the clock that hasn't worked since 4:48 on a day when it seemed time finally slowed to a stop, circles like the antique opal ring that Terry gave her, and then there's Terry: big-boned Boston bouncer at Club Zero

Hour located behind the Fenway, the hearty, Irish, shaved-redheaded overseer of the cage-dance bar crowd that he's paid to control with their wiry, bangled arms and pythonic, nylon-skinned legs sprouting from combat boots and silver platforms, and, look, there's Terry now: tight black T-shirt, hard body, jeans and silver-tipped boots, shaking down the clientele, running hands up thighs, over asses and groins, searching for nines and box-cutters and other shit the grungy, flannel-shirted boys (and lately the girls) try to get past, the geometry of Terry, the geometry of Jennifer, Jennifer Hampton, intersecting planes and lines and overlapping circles and then we turn to our assignment: *Graph the total area, spatial solidity, and utter leather morosis of Jennifer Hampton on a solid three dimensional plane (note: be sure to make use of the fifth axiom and point P)*, and to begin the assignment we use a blank sheet of paper, blank slate, start clean, pen and pencil, and we wager softly on the depending outcomes of logistical circumstance, positive relativism, apathia, we allow to coincide the Sunday morning that big-boned Terry Hogan woke up in Laura Huron's four-poster canopy bed, the brittle condom still biting around his flaccid manhood, his head a crescendo of constricting blood vessels, and at the same moment Jennifer Hampton pouring her morning urine into a clear chemical solution and then over the colored cardboard dipstick embossed with two tiny indicator circles, one pink, the other white, almost simultaneously swallowing three pregnancy-deterring circles, trying to make up for the three she missed last month after spending a Friday/Saturday/Sunday biking from Roxbury to Cape Cod with Miguel, but her Sunbeam clock above the dish-filled sink doesn't tell time anymore and Jennifer sends a letter to Roxbury, to Miguel in Roxbury, Miguel *from* Roxbury, now the slim-hipped hairdresser on Newbury Street, bi and beautiful, sideburns cut like coke, and the letter starts politely, calmly, *Hey there stranger*, then a few lines later, *Can you believe this is happening to me? I'm getting it done next week, hope I don't get shot by someone wearing a Save a Fetus for Jesus pin, guess I'm going to have to slow down, haven't used my brakes in so long, hope they still catch, wld love to hear from you, where you been? love Jennifer*, and if the Sunbeam clock above the dish-filled sink had still worked she'd have known that it was two-hundred-and-twenty-nine hours since she walked downtown to the corner of Derby and Congress and pulled the lip and fed the mouth of the mailbox a pink envelope addressed to Miguel de la Cruz of Humboldt Avenue in Roxbury, Massachusetts, who, at the exact moment when the mouth of the mailbox was being pulled by Jennifer's small, many-ringed, black-fingernailed hand, was asking another women, this one even smaller-boned than Jennifer but almost the same age (actually fourteen months younger, but he, Miguel, never asks, only hopes) to accompany him on a trip from Roxbury to Cape Cod, he says it'll be the best exercise she'll ever enjoy getting, and touches her arm on the very same spot where he touched Jennifer's for that crucial second longer than is necessary, and his pouty tight lips will finally spread east to west, and this girl, Veronica, fourteen months younger than Jennifer, Veronica Sheldon, a transplanted District of Columbian, will remember how her ex, Brian, Brian of South Boston, with his Leprechaun-tattooed shoulder, promised her romantic trips like the one she'll take with Miguel, down to the Cape or to Walden Pond or Revere Beach or somewhere, anywhere, just as long as she wouldn't leave him or cheat on him or look at other guys, and how his promises for romantic getaways became inter-textured with his promises to stop drinking until that Friday night last December when he opened up the side of her face, his diamond Claddagh-ringed fist catching her below the cheekbone, and now that pinkish-purple worm crawls across her cheek forever, but Miguel said she was beautiful, and that's more than anyone else ever said to Veronica Sheldon, and Jennifer's clock has hands that don't move and Jennifer's addressee, Miguel, will pedal next to Veronica Sheldon and the two of them will cross the Bourne Bridge together and not see passing them, *intersecting their radii,* the smoky green Saab of the doctor who first looked at Veronica's cheek the night Brian's fist left its mark, and Dr. Powers will speed his Saab from Harwichport back to Boston, a smoky green line segment darting from the center point of his world toward the circumference of another, speeding back to Boston, back to Beacon Hill, to give his daughter's college dorm-mate, Emma, twenty-seven years his junior, a gold tennis bracelet and dinner in the North End, and up on the fourth floor in an apartment across the street from the restaurant, across the street from Giovanni's, where Dr. Powers and Emma are planning the duplicities of their delicate new union, up on the fourth floor Leslie and Karen are stoned and sixty-nining, and Leslie moves her tongue in empty circles between Karen's labia majora, wishing Jennifer Hampton would just return her phone calls, but Leslie knows that Jennifer only sees the night they slept together after Club Zero Hour, the night Leslie had to spend an hour and a half to get her Astroglided fist wrist-deep inside Jennifer, Leslie knows that Jennifer Hampton only sees their night together as her obligatory college-feminist foray into the trendy lesbianism that's been written about so much lately in *The Phoenix* and *The Voice,* Leslie knows that small-boned, green-eyed Jennifer Hampton with her witchy pentagram tattoo on her slim Salem ankle only wanted to piss-off her ugly, shaven-headed, control freak, total breeder, bouncer boyfriend because he puts his hands way too far up women's skirts when he's working the door, Leslie knows that Jennifer is one of those total breeder girls who desperately want to be bi, really bi, like beautiful Miguel whom Leslie introduced to Jennifer in Boston, the day they were having double espressos and rolling Drum cigarettes, sitting on Newbury Street at the Armani sidewalk café, and Leslie knows that Miguel took one look at Jennifer's sad green eyes and her all-too-ripe twenty-year-old body and thought, *Mmmm, definite bike trip to the Cape*, and, to be honest, Leslie doesn't even believe Miguel is really bi, since for as long as she's known him he's never gone biking down the Cape with anyone but beautiful young girls, and, as for beautiful young girls, Leslie also knows that Jennifer blew her off that next night at Club Zero Hour so she could make her bouncer boyfriend jealous again, but this time with Miguel, not some dyke from the North End—*just return my fucking calls, bitch*—and although a non-subscriber to phallocentrism, Leslie will use a Jell-O-red dildo on Karen whose legs will be tied too far apart so that later when she is untied and gets up to use the bathroom she, Karen, will walk stiff and grimace like an old woman with arthritis, while in Salem, Massachusetts, the city where broom-straddling witches decorate refrigerator door magnets and the sides of police cars, in Salem, Massachusetts, Jennifer Hampton places a Nine Inch Nails CD into her Sony Discman, the silver circle refracting in her tobacco-stained fingers, and she won't remember that she was supposed to return one of Bull-dyke Leslie's two dozen manic messages—*she's such a drama queen*—she'll be rehearsing some new dance steps for the beer-glazed, tear-glazed eyes at Shelby's Slink Factory in front of her oak-framed mirror that she found in Marblehead in someone's trash, she will be thinking about Miguel and the baby that never was, and she will roll a tight Drum and decide to take a walk and think and write Miguel another letter, and she will see the October moon fat and round in the grape ZaRex sky, and this will invigorate her, make her feel consumed with a belief in fate, a belief that everything happens for a reason under that great glowing green-cheesed celestial sphere, and who says it's not the eye of the goddess? our mother in the night, able to pull the oceans away from the sands and up into the stars? who says it's not all going to work out in the end? who, other than Jennifer, after all, can control her own fate? and that's when Jennifer will see Anthony, Anthony the painter, Anthony the artist, who uses hollow-core bathroom doors in place of canvasses, and who stacks them down the cellar of his apartment building where his landlord, Raymond Callabrazio, will throw them out next week since he's been vowing to do so for months now to his wife, Sophia, who had her breasts enlarged and her nose jobbed last year and who, while during her stay in Salem Hospital, saw the smoky-green-Saabed Dr. Powers walk past her room every so often and although she never met him she considered him a very attractive gentlemen, but right now here's Anthony the painter, Anthony the artist, whose daytime job is bike courier and who delivered a white package last week to a man named Jules in Jamaica Plain for three hundred dollars, but Anthony didn't ask any questions, just delivered a package is all, a portion of which got cut up and split in half and distributed to a young dealer, Jason Barnard, who sold a portion of his portion to a queer named Miguel who works in some hair salon where Jason's other customer Karen Delmaro works, Karen who lives with her girlfriend, Leslie, in the North End across the street and four floors up from Giovanni's Restaurant, the present locus of love and linguine for Dr. Powers, but right now to the north of that spatio-temporal amorous cabal, right now, here comes Anthony the painter, Anthony the artist, coming right now toward Jennifer, walking slowly, left hand in pocket, in the right a cigarette glowing like a lit fuse, coming toward Jennifer Hampton from the direction of the college, scraps of fallen leaves skittering between the closing chasm of their collective steps and mutual paths, and Jennifer will look down, *avert her gaze*, as Anthony passes, she will see the dim splatters of paint on his black Doc Martens, and she will turn back as he passes but not say a word after seeing that he cut his ponytail off, and Jennifer will keep walking, as will Anthony, two integers, units of measure, unknown values and variables, maybe positive, maybe negative, void now to extrapolation, moving in opposite directions on a given line, distance compounding with every step, no backward glances now, and Jennifer will walk on until she ends up at the college, the buildings black this time of night, and across the street she will step into the college pizza shop, which is actually called College Pizza and Sub, still open, thank goddess, and Jennifer will order a slice of pepperoni and a small coffee, and sit at a brown Formica table and pull out her pouch and roll another cigarette, looking at her reflection to the left in the darkened front window of the shop, and begin to conceive another letter to Miguel, and that's when she will see Anthony, ponytailless, his paint-speckled Docs glowing extraterrestrially in the neon light, and Anthony will enter and stare up at the posted food prices and run his hand through his hair and feel around for the amputated limb of ponytail and then realize and reach farther down, as if to scratch the back of his neck, and he will pretend not to notice Jennifer Hampton, who at the same time is pretending not to notice Anthony, acting all preoccupied in getting her cigarette to roll just right, head bent down, fingers working the white paper into a fat, soon-to-be-delicious smoke, and Anthony will make his order, a small onion and mushroom, please, oh and hey, throw in a can of Diet Coke with that too, ah-ight? and the man behind the counter wearing a stained apron will bark back in broken English, small pizza-pie? and Anthony will say, no, no pie, thanks, just the pizza, to which the man behind the counter, head down now like Jennifer's, already spreading the toppings over the tomato-pasted dough, tossing the onions and mushrooms out like a dealer at a blackjack table, will say, oh ya, oh ya, okay, small pizza-pie for you, and Anthony will smile nervously and turn back to get a reality-check response from Jennifer whose head is still down like the man behind the counter, *the man behind the counter*, whose wife, Marta, is kneeling in front of a candle-lit religious shrine across town, her head down at that very moment, just like her husband's, just like Jennifer Hampton's, three heads all bent down at that very moment, three points of a triangle spreading out across the city, and Marta's head at one vertex bent down in prayer now, praying for her husband's fingers to get cut off in the salami slicer, and Marta, emotionally exhausted from working the late shift at the pizza shop after her husband, the man behind the counter, begins his affair with a chubby college freshman named Nicole, Marta will imagine one great day shooting and killing her husband, shooting him in the face, his head broken open and spilling over like a fabulous piñata, syrupy colors running all over the floor of the pizza shop, College Pizza and Sub, colors everywhere, on the tops of police cars and ambulances, on the walls and the cash register, and if Marta's lucky that night: on the blouse of that *puta* Nicole, colors running out of her husband's open head like the vibrant paints Anthony had used on those hollow-core bathroom doors, those doors which by that time, thanks to Raymond Callabrazio, will be forgotten in some dump, buried under a card table once belonging to the poet Lucie Brock-Broido, but Marta won't know any of this, won't know poets or paints, won't know guns or gun-dealers, won't even know Jason Barnard who could hook her up with any firearm she desired just by making a phone call to the pager of a West Indian called Toby, but Marta won't know the right equation for tracking Jason Barnard down, and soon Jennifer will be back with big-boned Terry after spending two-and-a-half artistic months with Anthony the painter, Anthony the artist, but right now here's Anthony sitting across from small-boned, white-faced Jennifer Hampton who is chipping bits of black polish off her fingernails, her head still down, a black pen lying across an open notebook, and Anthony will follow her uninterested lead and look down at his own hand, at the gray sprinkles of paint on his knuckles, and then over at Jennifer,

—Hey, weren't you in my figure-drawing class? he'll say, and Jennifer will snap her head up, and with the thespian acumen of DeNiro, feign surprise;

—Excuse me? she'll say, plucked brows arched, but eyes lidded with apathy, and Anthony will explain that he was um mistaken he thinks maybe, but he's sure he's seen her around uh maybe in Boston? and Jennifer will mention Club Zero Hour and how this guy she's um kinda like seein' but not for much longer is a doorman there, and Anthony will ask for some of her tobacco, getting up and joining her at her table in an unspoken gesture that communicates his gallant refusal to let her reach across the fluorescently-soaked, garlicly-odoriferous pizza shop, and she will ask him what happened to his ponytail, and he'll say he had a job interview and like he was getting like totally sick of it anyway, besides everyone has one now, even the assholes, and Jennifer will agree and smile, flashing the silver bar in her tongue, and Anthony will smile back, and they will eat pizza and drink coffee, smoke cigarettes and be sweetly ignorant like two people who are about to fuck for the first

time often are, and for the next eighty-two days big-boned
Terry will join Leslie and the legion of other phone callers
whose messages Jennifer won't return, and Terry will call
Miranda Kaiser from Swampscott who wears a *Jobs Not Jails* pin
on the front of her backpack and who volunteers planting
trees in a small playground in Roxbury, two streets over from
Humboldt Avenue, and in the next eighty-two days Terry
will give Miranda thirteen orgasms, two dozen roses, and
one case of Herpes Simplex Two, a disease miraculously not
transmitted to Jennifer Hampton, the contagium's progress
halted, cancelled out on her side of the supposition, her
graphed placement inside the text of this assignment, this
geometric assignment, this practice problem that asked us
to graph the total area of Jennifer Hampton, plotting points
like the naming of already-dead stars, and when the pizza
crusts lie splayed upon the silver tray, and the fat October
green-cheese moon glows outside the dark shop windows,
and Jennifer Hampton swallows two small circles down with
her last sip of coffee, and crumples another aborted letter
to Miguel, dropping it into the butt-filled ashtray, the man
behind the counter will clear his throat and say, we closing, we closing, and Jennifer and Anthony will stand and
stretch and then leave in search of latex circles and more
cigarettes, Anthony hoping his roommate, Hal, isn't still
up watching the Playboy Channel, the smell of sperm per-
meating the paneled room, discarded Kleenex by his feet,
and Jennifer will hope Anthony's not in an *orally generous
mood* tonight since she hasn't showered since this morning
and waxed since last week, and the outline of Jennifer and
Anthony will darken, then disappear into the tree-lined
expanse of Lafayette Street, and the man behind the counter
will move in front of the counter to clear their table, wiping it with a rag in broad, muscular circles, repeating the
words again to himself, we closing, we closing, we closing.

Man on Couch

Something inside me had died. While something else, *something other*, was dying to be born—dying to bloom and plume, there and then, as I sat in my sister's newly purchased luxury-loft condo in South Boston at her nondenominational Winter Solstice holiday party in her white semiglossed living room in the Seagrass Honey Weave Wingback Chair that I had shipped to her as a housewarming gift last summer from the Pottery Barn around the corner of my apartment on West Nineteenth. Sitting alone, I, just weeks before the turn of the millennium, trying to put Y2K out of mind, contemplating my sister's party guests and her hollow sheet-rocked walls and veneered entertainment center with a TV monitor playing an image of a yuletide log burning inside a fireplace; above the fireplace a wreath of holly in the shape of a pentagram and her green and red table-clothed table with upside-down red and green plastic cups, and a big glass bowl full of eggnog and ladle; and plates of chips and hummus and salsa and dips of white and yellow and green, just sitting there, I, alone, taking it all in, and drinking my Absolute Appletini, in the Seagrass Honey Weave Wingback Chair next to my sister's beige, somewhat stained, solid birch, obviously Ikea, couch. And there on the end of this couch was seated a man about my age, late thirties, but with a boyish face. Boyish, I say, as compared to my own ravaged, flesh-domed visage: a face that has had much toll taken, a face that has had all the boy blasted out of it. The body I am in, however, is strong, as anyone can observe under this leather vest; it is massive and sculpted and striated and hard; my crotch is full and heavy and hangs in two kidney-shaped bulges over the seam of my leather pants; my pectorals' nipples are pierced and fleshy and thick as a pencil's eraser, but my egg-shaped head and cracked-shell face is how my sister comes to call me Fester. My eyes dark and drooped and wrinkled, skin pocked from sand storms and Gulf War Syndrome and GWS-related eczema resulting in hair-loss of scalp, eyelash and brow, which this smudgy makeup and all the king's greasy brow pencils can't paint back together again. And then there was adolescent acne and several hospitalized bouts of alcohol poisoning and liver infections and some of the angry little cutting things I used to do with the sharp end of a drafting compass to these pustules. But despite all this hairless-headed dark gauntity, I still hold out the hope (out of reach though it may be, but what's a heaven for?) that someone somewhere might find something to adore in all this wreckage.

But going back, the boyish-faced man on the couch was wearing a nice shirt (button-up, no tie), nice T-shirt under it, too, nice, real nice, could just make out its soft teal collar, and some smart slacks and youthful footwear, perhaps too youthful for his age—the footwear style I see younger people wearing these days, a kind of stylish cross between sneaker and shoe: brown faux-leather like a shoe, but fashionably athletic like a sneaker, with European Soccer-inspired insignias and funny rave-ripe color combinations and toe styles reminiscent of bowling shoes or golf shoes or even the fashionable sport sneaker of my day: the Spot-bilt, which was the preferred sports shoe of the wealthy kids in my high school. Not the kind of footwear I'd ever be comfortable wearing. Never owned a pair of Spot-bilts or any of the funny fashionable stylish low-heeled shoes that when I was in high school my group of friends would have said fairies wore, such as Capezios or Candies for Men or the thin-soled shiny slick Italian shoe you'd see worn week after week on the Merv Griffin-produced television disco dance competition of the late-seventies, early eighties, *Dance Fever*, hosted in its first two seasons by Deney Terrio, the homosexual who later sued Merv Griffin for sexual harassment and who taught John Travolta his moves for the sleeper-hit motion picture of 1979, *Saturday Night Fever*, in which film's opening and establishing shots we are allowed to see only the shiny fashionable shoes on the strutting feet of the svelte young Travolta walking midday through Brooklyn, swinging a paint can, his long legs like a fine thoroughbred's striding, and as the camera slowly pulls back to a medium shot it seems to literally climb Travolta's young, svelte Italian-American body, almost having to slow down for a moment over the zippered speed bump of his packed and obviously quite large ethnic groin, and then up softly it seems the camera moves like a caress over his tight polyestered torso, up farther still over his rakishly unbuttoned shirt collar and hairy chest and indisputable-proof-of-God dimpled chin, until we are allowed finally to gaze upon the full mouth and large, vulnerable eyes of the actor's indescribably handsome, boyish yet mannish, insouciantly sensual face, just as Travolta's character, Tony Manero, is casting his own desiring, wanton gaze upon a pair of fashionable, shiny, presumably Italian-leather shoes. Our watching of his watching, the meta-moment of the watcher being watched, my telling you making my gaze watched, thrice gazed, gaze upon gaze upon gaze, a mirror of desire refracted and multiplied, desire like a fun house in which we lose all perspective and thus must, in order to escape, grope toward terrifyingly distorted bodies only to discover that those terrifying bodies are in fact our very own.

But going back, I don't hear people use that term that much these days. Think we must have got it from that Sabbath album we all listened to in junior high, tune called "Fairies Wear Boots." Should add into here I suppose that I wear boots, but not those pointy-toed, folded-cuff elf boots or the fashionable urban cowboy boot, those Dingos you'll sometimes see fairies wear, like if when say you're with a group of guys on the Cape, walking Provincetown's Commercial Street or hanging out late-night down in front of Spiritus, or even say in my own neighborhood of Chelsea or down in the Village on Christopher Street or during the high season at Fire Island or even alone walking along the West Side Highway with a half-pint bottle in one hand and a cigarette in the other, stumbling in your Timberlands, or, say, even back farther west from the highway, in the shadows of the those piers along the Hudson, say, during a low period in your life in the late nineteen eighties, just after you moved to New York and knew no one; were trying to figure a few things out, is all, trying to straighten some things in your head, before you went and enlisted—like some horse's ass—because you didn't think anything could happen to you from your own country, that the thing that would finally get you out of it all, as you had secretly wanted all along, would be the enemy's side, not yours; and then when you came back ugly but still regrettably alive nobody would even believe you; they just thought you suddenly, like overnight, became really ugly, just turned into this ugly thing, a six-foot-seven-inch ugly giant, nay, go ahead, say it, *monster* (for if they didn't say, their eyes did), and before there and then, you were standing by those piers all alone, as usual, you, under a dirty Manhattan moon, the smell of steaks from West Village bistros burning in the air that only hours earlier had sat rotting just north in the meat-packing district, the steely-stench-of-blood-and-death meat-packing district before it became the fashionable real estate district that now every architect in your firm except for you patronizes and actually requests to sit out of doors of in order to cut the tips off cigars and sip scotch; but way back then in the late eighties, you were all alone standing just south of there, that copy of *Closer* he gave you sticking out of the back pocket of your jeans, the boggy, mineral smell of the algaed scum rising from the river, standing there alone smoking, alone thinking, alone praying, alone, always, you, long, long after midnight—just as an example; I mean, if you look around you'll see them wearing those boots at some of those places, I would say. Not my taste, however. Give me Timberland work boots or Merrill hiking boots or, like, these jungle combat boots down here or even the Doc Marten boot—but only in basic black—the Doc Martens that come in the fashionable colors and slick trendy styles make my stomach turn, make me want to ralph. Could ralph just thinking about them. The kind of Doc Martens that when we were in high school we would have said were worn by Fagotty Andys. Those pearlescent red ones I'm thinking of, like Dorothy's ruby slippers, which, not sure if anyone knows this or not, but were designed by Gilbert Adrian for MGM, and were actually made in triplicate and had different soles affixed depending on the needs of the sound stage such as when layers of felt had to be glued to the bottoms because of the clacking sound they made on the hard surface of the yellow brick road during the big dance sequence; and a little known factoid about an assistant designer whose name has since fallen into oblivion but was commissioned to make a special pair that had rubber vaginas inserted inside for the

big-moneyed men with a taste for female feet, from MGM
who bankrolled the whole production. But I've seen shiny
blue ones too, one time, when I was getting my MArch at
MIT, this kid, a kid wearing a pair right outside of the
Fenway. Almost ralphed.

But going back, the guy sitting on the end of my sister's
couch: I thought he was with the people sharing the couch
with him, because he was making jokes and they were all
laughing, and they seemed to enjoy listening to him talk,
their beautiful perfect eyes glittering, perfect smiley mouths
all agape, drinks held aloft, rapt at every word, the smell of
pot coming in from the balcony, my sister sticking her head
in the ajar French door and asking if anyone wanted a hit;
and sometimes he did do funny imitations of people, some
of whom I knew, some of whom I didn't. He was very good
at these imitations. Some of the imitations required him to
sing and stand up and dance a little, which he did in what I
thought was a clever way. Like someone talented feigning a
lack of talent who was making fun of someone untalented
but who thought himself quite talented belting out a show
tune, and I should add into here that I'm pretty sure he was
doing a bit of Sondheim, something from *Company*, which
1970 production always seemed to me in terms of character-
development to have had its genesis in the work a young
23-year-old Sondheim did on the 1953 TV series *Topper*,
the show's protagonist Cosmo Topper being the archetype
for the overtly commitment-phobic and closetedly homo-
phobic and so-obviously gay, Robert; while with respect to
Company's hard-to-follow nonlinear style wherein narrative
segments and digressions kind of come and go without any
exposition and of which it is left to the audience to make
sense, it seems to have engendered its narrative strategy
in Sondheim's decades earlier deployment of ghosts who

assume the earthly form of a heterosexual couple named
George and Marion Kerby, who would literally pop in and
out of the ether around Cosmo Topper, and who, comfortable in their privileged heterosexual skin, were involved in
a continuous plot-line wherein every episode they would
try to get the uptight (read: *closeted*) Cosmo Topper to stop
worrying so much and to start living. And the man on the
couch was sending all this up kind of brilliantly, I thought,
inventing his own clever lyrics about closets and hangers
and hang-ups, lyrics that were in and of themselves funny
and ironic, but which were also, in a sort of overdetermined
mode, somehow also commenting on the semiotic distance
between the overt message of his lyrics and their ironic
subtext, which seemed both a simultaneous deconstruc-
tion and parody when considered in juxtaposition with
Sondheim's original lyrics, and in which ironic interstice
was to be found, I would argue, all the power of the man
on the couch's humor or, more precisely put, his wit. I had
a professor at UMass, not in my engineering program, but
a poet, philosopher, and aesthetician, who taught some
free electives I took, and who loved Sondheim and who,
when his wife wasn't home would play me and other guests
record albums and open many bottles of white zinfandel
(we all drank it by the cartons in those days), and would
end up sometimes weeping on his sofa in front of his fireplace (his sensitivities can not be overstated), explaining
how sad he was that he could not share this passion with
his own wife, who was a gender studies professor at the college, his wife was, and who had on far too many occasions
chided him for his sensitivities and aesthetic interests,
and who had expressed to him often, he related, how utterly bourgeois she thought Sondheim; and once, to me
alone, in the kitchen after her husband had fallen asleep,
his head drooped, the fire wavering sanguine behind his

beret, the copy of *Closer* he gave me deep in my back pocket where he'd slid it in himself, his wife, after she'd returned from a Hystory/Herstory curriculum-committee meeting, the manila folder's tab's affixed label needing two lines of minutely fonted text to signify this, expressed to me exactly what a bore she thought her husband's music and his wine and his big limp dick, as she mockingly and poutingly referred to it. "Doesn't matter how big it is if it can't get hard," she said. "Does wine do that to your dick?" she asked me. "Yes," I said, and stood up, my head hitting the chandelier above the table. His wife was also, my professor had said, a closeted Marxist. "Fucking freak," she said to my back as I walked through the door. I could hear her cigarette lighter scratch to flame.

But now leaning forward in my Seagrass Honey Weave Wingback chair toward the man on the couch, I began to smile and laugh along with everyone around me. Then the man on the couch noticed my interest and began talking to me, trying to include me in the couch conversation, which had spread to the people in the chairs next to me, not wingback though, more like these blond wood Ikea things, pretty to look at, but nothing that will last, but so these other people in the chairs whom I didn't know but the other people on the couch did were talking to one another about some other man not in attendance who was very, very ill but who, they said, was making a wonderful recovery, but whom neither the man on the couch nor I knew, and so the man and I had to make conversation one-on-one while the others talked, and he told me that he was not, in fact, with the couch people but that he had come alone, and when I told him I was the party-giver's brother he made another big display of his imitation skills and this time pretended to be a woman or a feminine-voiced man or just a feminine

man and said that he was going to have to speak to my sister
for keeping me a secret for so long, and did I simply love
living in Manhattan, and if I hadn't yet I positively had to
the very minute I returned after the holiday drop by his
favorite café that he missed so much now that he lived in
Massachusetts, and that was located a mere two blocks away
from Nineteenth Street, and when I went there I'd have to
ask Patrick to make me his famous lemongrass spirilina
chai macchiato, and then the man on the couch reached
over and felt my biceps.

I have well-defined biceps and thick arms in general.
When I was in basic, I had the record for most push-ups
and chin-ups, which push/pull method I should add into
here is the ideal approach to over all muscle conditioning. But not for growth. Not for arms like these. You want
growth, you're going to need roids. And protein powders
and supplements and other salt-based biological oral car-
riers that include bio-available and membrane permeable
nutrients, minerals, and substrates. I suppose I should
add into here that I did some roids in high school. Only a
few cycles during the season, but you know, we always went
to the championships, the turkey bowl, so we had to stay
huge, but I wasn't into it like some of the other guys I went
to high school with. Some of those guys were anabolized
beasts. Total roid heads. Roids'll do that to your head.
Like this guy Freddie Machico, whose girlfriend, Tammy,
I should add into here that I put it in her, I did put it in
her, everybody knew that I did, she told some people and
so did I, we both told, we didn't care, no don't-ask-don't-
tell policy for us, so yes, that's what I'm saying: I put it in
Tammy Sullivan about two months before they found her,
after missing for a couple days, in the trunk of Freddie's
Mercury. Nothing to do with me, or my putting it in her,

no causal connection. But that's my point: That's what I'm trying to say about the ill effects of roids on your head. Other problems too: Like later on Freddie Machico had a heart attack benching four-eighty in the gym at Walpole Cedar Junction Maximum Security. See, roids'll do that to your heart too. When they got the bar off Freddie's crushed windpipe, a guard tried mouth-to-mouth on Freddie, and when that didn't work, he poked a hole in his throat with a pen and even tried blowing into there, then stuck his thumb in the throat hole and tried blowing again on his mouth; and when Bobby Elcinott, who's not up at Cedar Junction but was in DYS with Freddie when they were kids, heard the story for the first time from Freddie's brother Ricky Machico at what Ricky Machico called his "Ricky Machico's Annual Fourth of July Southie Bar-B-Q," when we were all drinking beers and sitting on his lawn furniture, Bobby Elcinott heard this story and lifted his Budweiser can in his Budweiser-brand neoprene and foam cozy, and said that in some way it was a good thing that Freddie died, because if Freddie opened his eyes and saw that guard kissing his mouth with his thumb in his throat hole, shit, Freddie would've fucking killed that faggot, or got killed trying, that's how bad Freddie hated faggots, Bobby said. And everyone, including me, raised their Budweisers toasting both to Freddie's memory and to how much we hated faggots. One more thing about Freddie Machico: Worst case of ass acne I ever saw in my life. His ass had virulent red spots running deep into his olive-skinned ass crack, angry red dots mottled by his dark ass hair, dotting his muscular glutes like buckshot, and in the locker room at Iron Man, that's the gym where we all used to lift, Freddie would rub a shiny, translucent, asprin-smelling cream all over his muscular, olive-skinned, almost-cubistically constructed glutes, which were rock hard and fist-shaped and looked more like the glutes of a black man, which everybody knows tend to be genetically superior to the white man's. Just watch any Mr. Olympia contest or Mr. Universe or the Arnold Classic or the Joe Weider Invitational or the Iron Man Pro or even the Tournament of Champions Pro Figure or any of the local lightweight competitions that you'll sometimes find late at night on ESPN 4, and then pause your VCR's video tape or DVD player's disc or your TiVo or whatever and get up close in front of the TV screen and sit there for a while cross-legged and really study the glutes of the black man, notice their shape, the shadowy caverns, the striations, count them, get honest with them, learn that way the lesson of those glutes, and then compare them to the glutes of the white man and you will see.

Some of the people on the couch next to my chair got up and went to smoke on my sister's condo's balcony that overlooks the southeast part of the Southeast Expressway, and when they had clicked shut the imitation French door behind them and their heads through the glass were blots against a South Boston sky, my sister's six-foot-one-inch-tall head towering over the rest, the man on the couch turned all the way to face me and I was amazed suddenly at how blue his eyes were and how good his complexion was and how his full lips resembled those of a young John Travolta. He swiveled and then hopped in a seated position closer to me and put his nearly empty glass down on the glass coffee table's surface, and put both of his hands' fingers to his cheeks and said that my sister was the best stagehand he'd ever worked with, and that she could break down a set before the pizza got cold, and that he and all the other actors would positively go fetal, simply would not be capable of doing what they did every night without the great contributions made from the good hardworking people like my sister, and had I had a chance to check out her trophies and had I met her new friend Sally, who was a groupie my sister had met on the championship female arm-wrestling circuit, whose number two national ranking she has held for the past four years. My sister and I are both genetically blessed armswise.

So that's how we got onto the subject of testicular self-examinations. Something about the sick fellow they were discussing earlier, saying how he had lost his testicle and how he now always wears that yellow Lance Armstrong bracelet or something, and the man on the couch's and my eyes met and held on, lingering, not blinking, his full lips appearing to me a purply-pink blur beneath his two blue eyes, which now seemed to have flecks of hazel or green or light brown or even somehow appearing to be not even a color found in nature—all I can say is they were incredible to behold; and I gradually began to sense that we both were thinking the same thing: how awful it would be to have testicular cancer and to lose a testicle and how especially awful it would be given how avoidable it was if only we men, like women with their breasts, would take the time to understand how simple and easy and quick the self-exam really was. I mentioned to the man on the couch the great strides Colonel Norman Schwarzkopf had made to raise awareness of the prostate digital self-exam, and how I considered its digital inspection on par with the testicular self-exam, and again mentioned how back in basic Stormin' Norman was never considered a faggot or a queer or a bad man just because he digitally inspected his own almond-shaped gland which hangs or sits or perhaps more precisely lies wedged between the perineum and the ganglia mass just above the anus. The man on the couch agreed and made another of his very funny and now not

only well-loved by all, but almost expected by all, jokes, just
a little something to lighten the tension of cancer and our
brief candle's flame of mortality, this one about the colonel, whose name the man on the couch said reminded him
of *Hogan's Heroes* and he said that Stormin' Norman's name
sounded like something from that sitcom that ran from
1973 to 1976 and starred Bob Crane who may or may not
have been a faggot but was found dead in some hotel room,
most likely killed by a faggot, the news had said, after some
night of homo debauchery. Like that kid the *Globe* said they
just found in Hull out back of the armory up to the condos
there at Nantasket Beach, a dead kid with his head broken
open under a cracked cinder block, his pants around his
ankles, and a used condom hanging out of his dead bloody
anus, which upon closer inspection turned out to be his
actual anus, the condom did, not a condom at all but his
anus itself, hanging used and bloody and prolapsed and
redly bulging like a turnip or a baby crowning out of his
anus. I used to work out at Iron Man with some cops, and
one of them, Dave Duffy, who was in basic with me and is
now a statey was at the mall in Braintree yesterday with his
two little girls "getting mommy her gift," he said, "aren't
we?" And the little girls just stared way up at me, their eyes
kind of getting squinty from the lights above my head, and
then Dave and I got talking and he said that he was there
when they found the kid, and said that someone said when
they peeled his face from the underside of the brick, "Well,
that's what faggots get." Dave looked at his watch. "Listen,
have a great Christmas," he said, and I waved bye to the two
little girls, both of whom, each taking her father's hand,
began to cry.

All this talk about testicles and prostates started to make
me anxious. I felt the need for another drink. Whenever I

pray, God or higher power or whatever never takes away the feelings I ask him to as quickly as alcohol does. I've been waiting for years for an answer to my personal struggles, asking God or higher power or whatever to relieve me of a certain curse that he, it, or whatever has put upon me to test my character. A curse I will not name, but for which alcohol is quicker relief than prayer. Alcohol does not need to be prayed to or sought intercession of or asked or begged for mercy at night under the covers when you are so scared that the bed feels like a furnace or a tight sack around your face. Alcohol reads your mind, locates and attacks the fears. Takes them away so that you can, as a counselor back in basic told me, stop worrying so much and get on with the business of living. And here at my sister's party that was how I wanted to feel, like I was getting on with the business of living and though I didn't quite know it then, the alcohol did and that was why I knew I needed another drink. The man on the couch said that he was getting freaked out too by all this cancer talk and that, boy, didn't he also need another drink, let him tell me, and that he thought that the two of us should get some more Appletinis and after that, just to rid us both of this unnecessary worry, go into my sister's room and immediately examine our testicles and prostates.

My sister's room was dark except for a strawberry-scented candle she had burning in the little adjoining bathroom, whose door was open and through which opening wafted the soft warm smell of candle and stale pot and heavy leather and under all that the thin, uriney smell of my sister's patchouli. When my eyes adjusted to the tangerine dimness of the room, I and the man stood silently for a moment looking at her trophies and the photos of her arm-wrestling tournaments and newspaper clippings

and her welding gear and stagehand stuff. The crippling
anxiety and fear and terror of testicular and prostate cancer
abated somewhat from just knowing that this man whom I
had met this evening also shared my fears and concerns,
and this feeling of support and connection and brother-
hood overwhelmed me, and I was suddenly overcome with
the urge to examine my testicles and prostate immediately,
and I told the man to shut my sister's bedroom door and
to lock it for the sake of our feeling safe and comfortable
as women do at the gynecologist's. The man did as I asked.
From behind, I watched his perfect hair and normal-shaped
head atop his straight-backed-but-relaxed, wealthy-kid-in-
high-school posture as he stepped across the archipelago
of my sister's various floor rugs and unwashed laundry,
his glutes a glorious, chino'd thing. He shut the door and
locked it, and then he turned around to face me, but he
did not move from where he stood. I told him to come
over to the bed. He was a great deal shorter than I was
and not nearly as muscular and sculpted and striated and
hard. My leather-encased groin's bulge was bigger now on
the left side. The man stood looking up at me. His perfect hair's part was perfect, as if it had been drawn with a
ruler, cut with a compass. I told him to sit next to me on
my sister's comforter and batik bedspread. He dropped
down next to me, and then stared at his shoes. I told him
to look up at me. He only shrugged and picked at a nub of
batik fabric. Then he leaned back on his elbows, his belt
buckle had what appeared to be inlaid diamonds. But I
doubted they were what they appeared to be. His Adam's
apple ran up and down his throat, like a finger in there.
He put his hand to the side of his cheek. "What happened
to your face?" he said. His fingernails were perfectly
trimmed and his hands seemed carved from marble; they
were white and blue and pink, the skin fitting his hand's

bones perfectly. I knew that this man and I wanted the same thing: a healthy almond-shaped prostate and two cancer-free testicles. And I knew this would take time. I knew I might have to put one of my booted legs up over his shoulder and show him up close how it was done. I knew I would have to hold his hands as they went through each motion, offer words of encouragement, and demonstrate a great patience. And when he fumbled the job (and he would), I would have to bring his fingers back on track. He would want to watch me first. Learn that way the lesson of my hands. He might have thought we needed more light, but I believed it would be best to take this slowly in the dim, wavy, jack-o'-lantern shadows. His belt buckle twinkled. I said, "Do you have anything you want to say or ask me before we begin?"

And the man on the couch took his hand from his cheek and placed it on my hand. "My name," he said, "is Matthew."

"Matthew, the devil hath power," I said, putting his hand on the left side of my groin, "to assume—" But at this, he cleared his throat and took his hand away, slid it into his front pocket, and said, "If you'll pardon me, sir, but I hold not thee in thy hand, but rather the world—that sad stage, Gratiano, where every man must play a part." From his pocket he withdrew a condom. He held it up like he was examining a counterfeit bill. He squinted and rotated the condom in front of our faces. "And mine is a sad one." He dropped his chin on his chest and looked up at me. "Sad," he said, "but not tragic." He flipped his belt buckle open and undid his pants. He said, "And so be thine intents wicked or charitable, thou comest, sir," here he raised an eyebrow, "in such a questionable shape . . . blah, blah, I forget the rest of it, but I think there's something in there about a very potent devil who wants to abuse me. You know that part? You think you can play that part?" he said, and bit into the top of the condom wrapper.

"Well, Matthew," I said, "I'm not sure." I pulled his belt through his pant's belt loops, and wrapped it around my fist. "But I'm willing to give it a try."

Whatever, Forever

Bats need friends too, her T-shirt reads, Maya's T-shirt, the thirteenth of sixteen guilt-exonerating gifts that her dad has mailed her since last summer, since June 17th, 1994, since the divorce became final and he moved into the new house with his girlfriend, Bethany—his *girlfriend*—a phrase that, when she hears her fifty-five-year-old dad, over the phone, refer to his 34-year-old office partner that way, makes Maya want to gag, but *what-ever* with those two. Her father says please accept these gifts as his way of saying sorry, because he'd love to see her more often, but his practice and his new house are just taking up all his time, and now Bethany wants to go back to school for another degree, but she also wants so bad to have a baby, she's getting older, you know, and we have to start thinking about these things; but regardless of all that, he's been a little worried about Maya, her mother called him last week from Taos and said she hasn't heard from Maya in a few weeks, said Maya hasn't been returning her phone calls, is something going on with Maya?, blah, blah, blah, but her dad was so glad to hear that Maya liked the bat T-shirt, it warms his heart, and he thought of her, of course, as he and Bethany explored those caves, learning all about the bats, Maya's favorite subject, he says all buddy-buddy-daddy-daughter, and someday Maya absolutely has to join them for a visit there, because he'd really love for Maya to get to know Bethany a little bit better, because she's said on many occasions that she's very interested in having a real relationship with Maya, but, as a counselor to young people in crisis, Bethany knows exactly how Maya feels, she has no intention of trying to replace Maya's mother; she respects Maya's need to be alone right now, we both do, honey, because, her father says, they both know how busy people can be, people do have lives, after all, her father says, but then, well, he guesses Maya knows all about that, what with his being so busy with the new house these days and Maya's mother taking off to New Mexico like she did with that Helen friend of hers in tow, but he doesn't want Maya ever to forget that he loves Maya more than anything and misses her and wishes they could see each other more often, she should not hesitate to call him whenever she needs anything, promise? Whatever with those two. But indeed the bat T-shirt does rock, it's already got a few small holes and some black stains from her Manic Panic hair dye, and it's the perfect sleeve length to reveal Maya's sleeve tattoos: on her right arm: the old Vegas strip of Fremont Street set against a backdrop of casino chips and many colored dice; and on her left: twelve different species of bats set against a dreary midnight sky full of star-shaped stars, and Maya's had the T-shirt for only a few months, but she wears it all the time, like even sleeps in it and then wears it the next day without washing it, so it smells a little like vinegar and garlic—a body odor she delights in inhaling; she wears it so often not because her dad gave it to her, *please*, but rather because it has this really cute cartoon bat hanging upside down from a Gothic font which reads *Carlsbad Caverns*, and because, as everyone knows, Maya loves bats, loves everything about them, and not—as most people think—because she's into quote-unquote the goth scene, but because bats have the word survivor inscribed

into their DNA, genes of brutal evolutionary tenacity he-
lixing around their cute little molecule stems—goddess
gracious, she just loves them, and she knows everything
about them, too, everything: their sleeping habits, their
breeding practices, their food and feeding rituals, and the
way that bats relate to other animals—and to humans too,
she knows it all and not only can but will relate it to you as
she does so often to her friends in this really breathless way
she has, a sort of raspy, staccato celerity she possesses, a
rhythm that infects her speech (her *speech patterns*, as her
father, the clinical psychologist, calls them), it's the way
Maya has always talked since she was a little girl, bursting
into the wide open spaces of a new idea, then digressing
off of that idea, and then, all excited, getting a new idea,
interrupting her own digression, saying: "*Oh, wait, no, but
then there's also this. . . ,*" Maya having a sudden epiphany, Maya
needing to get it all out at once, declining through her
digressions like Diamanda Galas glides through vocal
ranges, winding and winding down the widening gyre of
her thoughts with vertiginous torque—a kinetic style really,
as if her sentences never end, as if she never uses periods,
her sentences just running on like bats flying away up into
the night sky, then swooping back down low, just above your
head, confusing you, putting you off your game, then up
she flies again, a great swarm of up, a great up of swarm;
and she knows she does this; it's not like someone has di-
agnosed this tendency; she's aware, and in fact, secretly,
she kind of does it on purpose, because she feels it's a part
of her identity somehow, her worldview, her caffeinated
cosmology, but most of all she sees it like an accessory to
go with that most elemental outfit of Maya's: her own body;
because the deal is, she's a small girl, she calls herself a stick
chick, only five-feet-one, a hundred pounds, and when she
goes off on one of her rant-rages it seems like her metabo-

lism has taken over speech, her hands and face getting twitchy and manic, vibrating to the music of her own spheres, as she stands there shaking and talking and frowning and waving, in her black combat boots and black tights and torn black skirt and black leather coat and black lipstick, and black eyeliner and black hair, some people say she looks like Robert Smith, but she prefers Ian McCulloch, but don't get her wrong, she loves The Cure, maybe even more than the Bunnymen, something in Smith's lyrics making her feel sane, or rather feel like she's not as insane as some people make her feel—*Oh, wait, no, but then there's also this:* little dots of black polish on the nails of her tiny bitten-nubby fingertips, but she doesn't care that she's got shitty finger-nails, only breeders and lipstick girls care about that, except that she wouldn't mind a nice set of claws, claws like her winged friends have, claws that could hold onto ledges of dizzying height, like the stone belfry of Old Salem Church, from which foggy perch she could peer down upon her entire Witch City, peer down upon Salem Harbor with the hillside cemetery of Marblehead off across that dark water, peer down upon the old lighthouse overlooking the salty mouth of the Atlantic, down upon the dry-splintered eaves of the House of Seven Gables, down even to Swampscott, to the gallows there where, contrary to popular knowledge, were hanged the wise women of her township, the women who did not need men, claws that could act as protection, as weapons, while she flies through the night air, her out-stretched wings a dark sail billowing above, the moon be-hind a flaming penumbra, claws that could scrape down a lover's back, down even (yes, she wasn't afraid to say the name) down Angie Kosinski's back, Angie Kosinski, (there she said it), but Angie won't be around any longer, not anymore, because she believes Maya uses people, eats people up, drains them like a vampire, or worse: like an artist,

just cycles through people, feeds off them until she's bloated
blood full, then finds another host, but, fine, if that's what
Angie Kosinski thinks, then she can think it, because Maya
knows better, knows herself better than Angie ever will,
and yet, one time, toward the end, Angie had claimed that
she understood Maya better than Maya understood herself,
which of course is total bullshit, on so many levels, one
being that of hubris, that she would actually claim such a
gift, the gift of inner sight, the gift of the goddess, the
second being that she actually had the ovaries to utter such
total crap aloud to Maya's face, like without assuming it
wouldn't infuriate Maya, infuriate the shit out of her because the one thing Maya cannot stand, positively cannot
abide, will punch the wall right next to someone's head if
they even so much as try, is when anyone thinks they understand Maya, thinks they got her figured out, like those
pages in the DSM IV that when she was in high school her
dad used to put little pink Post-it stickies on so that Maya
could be better acquainted with terms like narcissism,
anxiety disorder, ADHD, sexual addiction, relationship
addiction, codependency, whatever with all that, but then
that's Angie Kosinski—the great knower of Maya, under-
stander of all that is Maya; and that's why Maya's glad she's
gone, because now the apartment is cleaner and patchouli-
free, now there's more vodka left in the freezer, now she
can bring girls home whenever she wants, although she
hasn't actually been with anyone seriously since Angie left,
but last night she found the green wool socks that she'd
acquired the night she first met Angie in Boston on Lans-
downe Street, that October night when Skinny Puppy played
a Halloween show, and Maya had just bought the Skinny
Puppy VHS video collection at Newbury Comics the night
before, and she was talking about that new purchase to this
girl named Loretta DeFazio, whom everyone called Laverne,

because she was this total 50s girl, a real rockabilly chick, with short black bangs and a black satin bowling jacket with an image of Bettie Page on the back, Bettie's hands raised above a conflagration of orange flame in which she knelt, Bettie's face the spitting image of Laverne's, and Maya actually had a mini-crush on Laverne that night, crushed out on her white-pancake-skinned face and the barely visible plucked brows and those blood-red lips amid all that white foundation, dear goddess, but that mini-crush was soon to fade, she was getting tired of the rockabilly scene, and in the coincidental synchronicity of someone torn between two pop-cultural aesthetics, that was the exact night she met grunge-girl Angie Kosinski—auburn-haired, green-eyed, nonrockabilly, Seattle-style hippy-chick, small-boned like Maya, with an ungodly affection for the band Hole. Angie came up next to Laverne, wobbling a bit in her big hiking boots and old floral skirt, holding a cocktail, and wearing a Carpe Scrotum pin on her frayed flannel shirt, and Maya had left off the topic of Skinny Puppy now, and was boasting about her most recent prized purchase, the entire series of *Twin Peaks* on VHS, and Maya was dishing all this to Laverne, when Angie Kosinski interrupted and said in almost slow motion, totally fucking up the speed-metal tempo of Maya's diatribe, Angie held up her many-ringed hand and slowly slurred: "Wait a minute, wait a minute, hold it. Did you say *Twin Peaks*? Oh my God, I so totally love *Twin Peaks*." And then Angie closed her eyes, put her hand over on her chest and said that she simply frickin' loved *Twin Peaks* and oh my God especially that frickin' Kyle; and Maya made a weird face that Angie ignored, because Angie knew what Maya was hinting at, but Angie Kosinski, at that time, wasn't all the way in or out of any closet, so for a while Angie was all about pretending she never caught Maya's many references to that alternative lifestyle, but so as to push Angie's buttons a little Maya said, well, she *simply frickin' loved* Lara Flynn Boyle, and Angie merely smiled, looked down, and twirled her plastic straw around inside her plastic cup that looked like it was full of a lot of cranberry juice and very little vodka, but when Angie offered Maya a sip, Maya winced and said, *Damn that's strong!*, and Angie showed her the pint of vodka in her backpack, and then Angie got so drunk that night that later, when they were back at Maya's place and making out on her futon, Angie actually puked, like totally threw up in Maya's mouth, mostly vodka though, nothing chunky, Angie later apologizing and claiming to have been so dizzy that she absolutely couldn't pull herself away because she thought that moving even just a little bit would surely make her vomit, her head spinning and throbbing, and but then it came up anyway, and Maya yanked her head away so fast that her neck was stiff for days, but she toweled up the mess, wiping Angie's mouth and her own, then tossing the towel into the giant dark Hefty bag that Maya kept slumped for way too long in the corner of her kitchen, and when she came back into the living room, she stood and looked down at Angie passed-out on the floor, her flannel shirt unbuttoned, her purple bra still attached above those freckled ribs, her throat arched up, exposing the dip and cream curve of her neck, and then Maya got an idea, she knelt down on the floor next to Angie's head and put her fingers to Angie's lips, holding them there, touching their puffy softness lightly, then slowly she put a finger inside Angie's lips, rubbing her front teeth and then beyond them to her tongue, all the while Angie never budging; and then Maya reached out, and began slowly, incrementally, to lift Angie's skirt—just a little, at first, just snooping around, pulling it finally all the way up—then she got down and untied the laces of Angie's big hiking boots, tugging each one off, then peeling down the clammy green wool socks and then, in one smooth determined motion, she pulled Angie's underwear down her legs, releasing into the room Angie's hirsute scarlet diadem, *Damn, this chick is hairy,* Maya thought, and then she put the same finger she had just used as a tongue depressor into her own mouth, it tasting vaguely of something bitter and acidic, but Maya was way too drunk to care, and so she licked her finger all over, leaving a drop of spit shiny on her little black fingernail, and then carefully, stealthily, never taking her eyes off Angie's eyes which never opened, Maya put that saliva-wetted finger into all that red bush, but she contacted bone sooner than she imagined, and Maya realized that Angie's pubic bone bulged out over her softer parts like a cliff above a cave, and then Maya traced her finger down the curve of that bone, and farther down still to that nub of reticent tissue so full of shy remembrance, and all at once a real physiological wonder presented itself to Maya, something about Angie down there was larger than Maya had expected, so she took her fingers and parted all that hair, and, when she did this, lordy lord, she saw that this girl, Angie Kosinski, was not a girl at all, but some marvelously constructed woodland nymphic hermaphrodite or something—but no, wait, not a hermaphrodite, Maya decided, but there was something branching off of Angie down there; where Maya had only a little button, Angie had what seemed to be a thumb, and so Maya moved aside more of the flesh and realized that Angie Kosinski wasn't quite like any girl she had ever been with, and something stirred inside Maya, deep inside Maya; she looked again at Angie's closed eyes, the smudges and streaks of eyeliner, her lipstick smeary from their vomity kisses, and then all at once down Maya went, swooped down really, so hungry was she to taste this little mound of Angie, her tongue feeling out the bump of Angie, that firm but

tender sovereign, and she did this for a while, got lost in
the activity, and soon all this attention had a sobering effect on the passed-out Angie: Maya saw her open her eyes,
yet when she looked again they were closed, but Angie was
fooling no one that night because this passed-out girl began
raising her hips with every push and shove of Maya's mouth,
raising her hips and pushing back into Maya's pushy face,
getting ready, getting everything aligned, because, as she
told Maya later, Angie realized to Angie's great surprise
that Maya was really good at this, and she realized also that
she, Angie Maria Kosinski—of Salem, Massachusetts,
daughter of a police officer and an elementary school
teacher, baptized and confirmed out of the Church of the
Holy Mother, a once highly decorated Brownie and Girl
Scout, a much sought-after dog-walker, a knitter of scarves
and hats for friends' birthdays, president of the Massachusetts chapter of the Hole fan club—she, Angie Kosinski,
realized that she was about to come on another girl's tongue,
and along with this realization came a faint wave of giggles;
she wanted to laugh, not because it was funny, but laugh
because it felt so good, laugh because she just couldn't believe how frickin' talented Maya was at this, Maya was like
a total frickin' pro, like a maestro standing behind her
lectern, her tongue waving like a baton in a furious hand,
directing the rhythm of Angie's orchestra down there, and
all of Angie's musical nerve endings now dutifully followed
their conductor, picking up the tempo and getting ready
for the great crescendo; and for some reason the lyrics to
that song from *Heart* came into her head: *He's a magic man,
mama / He got the magic hands,* and Angie wanted to laugh again,
but Maya was now orchestrating something truly amazing,
and the fireworks began blazing behind her eyes, and Angie
tightened those closed eyes and concentrated, got into the
rhythm, and everything was set to go: the feeling of being

held between this girl's lips, the ticklish feeling of Maya's dye-damaged hair between her thighs, the just right placement of Maya's fingers, and then all at once, just as Angie was ready to let go, Maya stopped—just stopped—Maya then climbing up to Angie, lying down next to Angie, and slowly putting a deep kiss onto Angie's mouth, but Angie—now most certainly *not* passed out—took Maya's hand and put it back to work, and with a little concentration, Angie was back in the game, but this time she didn't want to giggle, this time she wanted to be hugged, and indeed Maya's other arm was under Angie's head, and Angie nestled into that slender tattooed nook, tensed her hips once again, and tried to refocus, to gather back up that gathering storm that had almost gone out to sea; and Maya, with her hand still working, leaning up now on one elbow, brushed back Angie's hair and softly kissed her ear, and Angie's breathing was shallow and quick and she was now moving her hips up and down against Maya's palm, and then, because she needed to let Maya know she was fully there with her now, her sister now, her girl, Angie uttered those three cosmic words, words that perhaps could be heard coming off the mouths of lovers all over the world at that very moment, words that were not even words but the breath of words, words of both poetry and prose, of lyricism and mysticism, of composition and journalism, words of both submission and agency, words that to a foreigner could be called idiomatic, three words that Angie whispered into Maya's hot face: *I'm gonna come*, and the whisper became a moan and the moan became song and the song became a howl, a throaty roar, a keening lamentation, a diaphragmatic proclamation, as if she had just been given truly tragic news, a deep wailing really, and then she said one more thing to Maya, "Fucking kiss me"—and all at once Maya opened her mouth, leaned down and bit deep into the side of Angie's creamy curved throat, and then Angie's moans of lust became a scream which became a shriek and with all the power she had, Angie reached up and grabbed Maya's hair, and with the adrenalinized strength that only mothers of trapped babies possess, positively flipped Maya over by the roots of her hair, a basic judo move, really, a counter-balancing of weight, something her father had taught her, and Maya went hollering all the way over her, a scream coming across the sky, and Maya landed hard on her side, her hips crashing onto the wood-planked floor, and Angie, drunk no longer, whipped up onto her knees and swept back her hair and in the same action stood up and stumbled back, falling against Maya's entertainment center, the TV toppling over, the VCR crashing, and the *Twin Peaks* tapes skittering across the floor, and Maya just watched, watched Angie wheeling around the room, naked except for her bra, and actually the bite was really small, just a flesh wound, but Maya could see that it was bright red, even from this far across the room, and Angie was staring at her hand, at the blood on her hand, and Maya was staring at Angie, who seemed now certainly sober and totally pissed, a fury made apparent by the words she was spitting: *crazy fucking bitch*, *sick cunt*; and then she flew back across the room at Maya, who covered up now, wrapped her arms around her head and curled up like a slug, Maya feeling her hair being pulled and twisted, a flurry of Angie's bare feet against her back, and then added to that fury she felt knees and fists and fingernails and elbows and even the wet of tears—or was that blood?—and then she felt everything stop. Two weeks later, Angie moved in. Go figure. But that's just the way Maya's life was spinning out its web in those days, Angie moved into the bat cave for three long months, and then one day, Maya came home and Angie's stuff was gone, no trace of Angie except for the green wool socks that Maya had stolen, but, hey, *whatever* with her, life goes on, and that weekend Maya went to a bar called Local 159, with Laverne, who would leave Boston for New York the following autumn and study creative writing in Greenwich Village and write stories about Maya, who the following spring would be found hanging from a pipe in her bathroom, Maya's black-rimmed eyes searching the ceiling tiles for two days before they cut her down, Maya's dad calling what friends of Maya's he could track down, offering her possessions to peruse if they wanted them before being given away; Laverne snagging the bat T-shirt, the smell of Maya still present (or so Laverne imagined); Laverne changing Maya's name in her stories, but not much else. But so that night at Local 159, while Laverne was playing pool with some side-burned guys screaming Johnny Cash lyrics, Maya gave her number to a bartender there named Jules, who never called her, but with whom she made out in the employee bathroom and into whose neck she also directed those teeth of hers, not breaking flesh this time, but really biting on, and Jules moaned and breathed in quick through gritted teeth, her knees buckling beneath her as she leaned against the bathroom wall for support, and, like Angie, pulled Maya's hair to finally, but sensually, unhook those little fangs, and later she set Maya up with a free beer, for which Maya tipped her three bucks along with her phone number, but to be sure: Maya really had a good vibe about Jules, and she felt that Jules really dug her too, because after this moment of porcelain intimacy and complimentary beer, Jules fell silent behind the bar, listening to the song Maya had just put on the jukebox, spinning a bottle opener around her middle finger, Jules looking reflective, sort of wistful, Maya thought: a beautiful bi-curious bartender with a big hickey and a bursting heart, standing there against the cash register, as The Cure blared over the bar's sound system, Robert

Smith singing about how he knew he was wrong when he said it was true that it couldn't be him and be her in between without you, *without you*, perhaps Jules thought she had opened herself up too early to Maya, given herself away too easily, but Maya needed Jules to know that that was exactly all she ever wanted from someone, that Maya would also give herself over completely if someone would just give themselves to her completely, not hold back, not bullshit her and play her and abandon her and leave her hanging, alone, like some sad bat in a damp, dark cave, and Maya wanted to say this to Jules that night, so she held her eyes on Jules and when she looked up again, Maya smiled at her, winked, took a sip of beer, it was all she could muster; cool, cool Maya, outwardly chill, but inwardly swooning and falling crushingly in love with this Jules, all memory of Angie seemingly erased in that employee bathroom, and then later that night, north of Local 159, north of Boston, in that city of witches where midwives and old crones paid a steep price for their desire to be different, later that night in her Salem apartment, alone in bed, Maya rolled over, hugged her knees, and murmured Jules's name into her pillow, her eyes closed, her stomach empty, she said the name over and over as she began to pass out, mumbling it like a slurry prayer upon her lips (yes, like a prayer, OK?, because, whether you believe it or not, it did actually make her feel better just to intone Jules's name), amid drool and bedspins and thumping headache, and then, like any self-respecting woman who gets blown off, she waited a whole week before going back to Local 159 and seeing Jules again, saying, *"Oh hi, yeah, um wait, it's Jules, right?"* to which Jules said, Sorry she hadn't called, she was like so busy this week, but she totally was planning on calling Maya next week like when her shit got less hectic, and Maya again was trying to act cool, a little aloof, nodding, smiling her crooked-toothed smile, but all the while as Jules spewed her excuses, Maya kept promising herself that she would, at the very first opportunity this evening, walk away, just go on, go on, and walk the fuck out of this bar and never come back again, never, ever—fuck this girl—who does she think she is, Maya would never sink so low as to return to ogle that fucking bitch across the bar, fuck her, never going to give her the pleasure of knowing how Maya feels about her, a heart of stone was Maya's now, she was through needing people, finished, finito, that was the end of it, totally going to cut Jules off, never going to talk to her again, never, ever, not in this lifetime, nope, uh-uh . . . not, that is, unless Jules called her, but—and this was a gigantic *but*—Jules would have to call her *within the next week*, like she totally said she was planning to do, because maybe, who knows, just maybe, she really has been super-busy, everyone can't be as available as Maya, she supposes, perhaps she'll give Jules one more chance, but only one, seriously, she means it, only one more, because people can be busy, after all, like her father said, people do have lives. Maya knows all about that.

Annus Horribilis, or The Carpenter, or Cal

Wherein how Jillian Hibnitz had fantasized off and on since girlhood about one day finding a boyfriend/husband-to-be who was a carpenter. It would be one of those epic old-fashioned love stories she would tell her children and grandchildren and great-grandchildren all gathered around her on that wrap-around porch in Vermont; her bountiful offspring all harvested—she would tell them, looking each offspring straight in the eye—from that potent male seed extracted in matrimonial union from the carpenter's fertile loin, Jillian Hibnitz the rich soil into which that seed was planted. *(Note: Maybe don't use real name, like workshop last time said was distracting. Fictionalize!)*

Wherein how *Jessica Henry* had fantasized off and on since girlhood about one day finding a boyfriend/husband-to-be who was a carpenter. Traditional narrative elements of biographical cause and effect come into play here for the curious reader only somewhat. For it was neither her father—whose job had to do with computers and who worked from home in the refinished paneled basement, and whom she saw at night and on weekends when he emerged in his bathrobe and boxers from the cellar door by the kitchen's pantry area, the stale-ashtray stench of his body filling the room (she'd wished he had more of a dad-job, anything where he wore pants and left the house once in a while and laughed with other men and came home at night and hugged her mother out of a pent-up need from being away from her all day)—nor any other primary male care-taker or role model or domestic presence that served as the source material or back-story for this fantasy. Rather, it was the boy from the other side of the tracks. As in literally. Jessica's family lived off of Route 114 in Salem, just east of Danvers, on the west side of the Boston-Rockport rail-road line, the train tracks running along the border of her backyard. On the other side lived the boy whose name she never knew, a boy—whom Jessica noticed for the first time from her bedroom window one raw and blustery Thanks-giving her sophomore year at Gallows Hill High—in his backyard, across the tracks, working on two flaming yellow saw horses, assembling what appeared to be a mantel for a fireplace, a white molded flare of wood. Working outside with his hands, no gloves, wearing faded jeans and work boots, a red flannel shirt unbuttoned, its tail whipping around his lean waist, sleeves rolled up, and what seemed to be a white thermal long underwear shirt underneath, sleeves of which not rolled. Flowing in the percussive wind, keeping time rhythmically with the shirttails, was his hair, long and dark, thick, sometimes at certain angles Christ-like, sometimes undulating like heat waves before a winter window. For it was only in winter that the trees afforded a view; summers she burned to catch even a glimpse of him through lush green leaves. (Note: Maybe cut some of what the bitch in wksp called "romance-novel descriptions of men.")

Wherein how Jessica Henry had fantasized off and on since girlhood about one day finding a boyfriend/husband-to-be who was a carpenter, a dream ignited early in life from crush on boy across the tracks. And wherein how this occasionally occurring fantasy sparked early her tender tinder and caught fire, burning throughout her difficult gangly-legged, flat-chested, rotini-haired, combat-booted, black-fingernailed, plaid-miniskirted, torn-fishnetted, cafeteria-intimidated, locker room-phobic, boy-petrified, bookish adolescence at Gallows Hill High School, only a football field and faculty parking lot away from where those unjustly accused witches swung—sisters in persecution all, averred shy, awkward Jessica. She took strength in their story. Indeed she saw herself a part of that tradition: *Jessica Henry*, self-proclaimed white witch; herbal healer of family pets; she of the pentagram-emblazoned T-shirt and necklace and necklace and rings and tattoo (right shoulder); a high school convert to Wicca; dabbler in earth religions; reader of Mary Daly; frequent invoker of term "goddess"; pierced of ear, eyebrow, labret, and septum; proud displayer of patch on backpack which reads "Eco-Terrorist"; often seen writing in small black Moleskine journal at the Derby Wharf lighthouse, a spot that affords the best view of The House of Seven Gables—her muse, her fascination, her port-of-call. *(Note: Maybe cut back on what that Cormac McCarthy wksp wannabe assfuck called my "clichéd Salem-setting-overkill.")*

Wherein how Jessica Henry had fantasized off and on since girlhood about one day finding a boyfriend/husband-to-be who was a carpenter. And wherein how the fires of wish-craft would pop and crackle and flare and spread even more wildly when she moved to New York for four more years of schooling as an English major at Sarah Lawrence. Finally conflagrating the majority of her imaginative life upon graduation, wherein soon thereafter she was jobless, anxiety-ridden, depressed, and overmedicating, all without the support of her therapist, Dr. Athene ("Tina") Kristophoros of Swampscott, she of the soothing music, ocean-views, and modern-art-inspired Kleenex boxes. And wherein how Jessica Henry slept nights on her friend Miriam's couch in Greenpoint, Brooklyn, during a suffocatingly humid July, without A/C, while seeking employment. And wherein how during that infernal July, the carpenter fantasy had served to soothe her panic-attacks, and thus by sheer utilitarian value the fantasy had reached higher temperatures, raging on yet ever-brighter through the next year and a half, working as the receptionist at Briny and Bilge Software Solutions, in midtown Manhattan, her cubicle just in front of the entrance door, so close that anyone coming through that door into B & B's 17th-floor office would bang Jessica's cubicle's front panel, causing her dragon and devil and angel knickknacks and photos and pins and dream-catchers and seashells and crystals to either fall or jostle. And wherein how she, Jessica, after much Craigslist-ed disappointment, finally found an apartment in the borough of Queens, with two roommates. *(Note: Here describe roommate Rupa's control-freak rules about common-room cleanliness and procedural dishwashing directions even though she spends many of her nights in Astoria with boyfriend Sanjay, leaving Jessica alone with other roommate, Morgana. Here describe Morgana's shrill vibrato sex-lowering at five in the morning and her sex partners who—after battering Morgana percussively against the headboard of her bed and by extension the adjacent wall behind that headboard and, thus, by architectural extension, the wall behind the headboard of Jessica Henry's bed—would then stumble loudly down the hallway, and after extricating their penises from their Morgana-drenched condoms, would then drop said condoms to float fat and long and bloated and opaque in the unflushed yellow toilet water, getting apple-juice-dark drops of urine on the toilet seat and tiled bathroom floor —Note on note: Careful not to offend and/or alienate reader.)* And wherein how soon thereafter finding said apartment, Jessica Henry, full to

repletion with stories of that horrible year, registered for
an introductory fiction writing workshop at the 92nd Street
Y in order to express in a work of fiction the sadness and
keening loneliness she felt. For she desperately wanted to
write a story that people would one day not only read, but
be psychologically transformed by and spiritually healed
from and hope-renewed as a result of. She wanted her story
to save lives.

And wherein how in this fiction writing workshop
Jessica Henry would write stories only about the carpenter or of her beloved former township of Salem. What her
fellow workshop mates did not know, however, was how
powerful—nay, how plaited into the very helices of her
DNA—the carpenter fantasy had become, how the great
conflict in her life was this life-saving, anxiety-reducing,
depression-abating obsession. It went beyond mere psychic
balm; it ultimately eclipsed all of Jessica Henry's feelings
about the opposite sex, to such an extent that when she was
on "real life" dates with "real life" boys, she would, as Tina
called it, *dissociate*, float away mentally from her barstool or
food-court table and begin thinking about, or "fixating"
on the carpenter. And lately it had begun to happen more
and more often, even once a couple of months ago, at this
guitarist Jason Trimamore's apartment—while she and he
were totally *in flagrante delicto!* In fact, Jessica found that *in
flagrante delicto* was one of the best times to fantasize about
the carpenter.

It felt good to think—and write—about the carpenter.
In fact, she recently finished the first draft of a story based
on their first meeting: which would take place at the Righ-
teous Ways Food Co-op in Greenpoint, and wherein, amid
that setting, the carpenter would be shopping for PETA-

approved hair shampoo and organic bok choy (*Note: Maybe capitalize his name?*) And wherein how The Carpenter would be tall and lean, with longish, thick, wavy, dark, clean hair, traditionally handsome in that rugged and tough-looking way, but also super cu— (*Note: Should or should not use the word "cute"? Maybe "cute" would make story sound chick-litty; besides it's too "tell-ish"; try to find fresh ways to "show" him—maybe more provocative adjectives.*)

And wherein how The Carpenter would be tall and lean, with longish, thick, wavy, dark, clean hair, traditionally handsome in that rugged and tough-looking way, but also a thigh-spreadingly, labia-quiveringly, clitoris-engorgingly, g-spot-locatingly, almost-inappropriately-sexualized man (*Note: Too much? Consider cuts.*) with well-shaped hands and amazing hazel eyes, staring out from between strands of non-animal-tested shampooed and conditioned hair wisping out under his blue hemp bandana. And wherein how this Carpenter would be the new owner of a rambling old house in Vermont (*Note: Insert scene/narrative summary? He tells her all this, carries her groceries, as they stroll back from the food co-op to the apartment that he keeps in Brooklyn*) that he had just bought for a song and on weekends was fixing up and converting into an eco-friendly house with sustainability features such as rainwater collection, gray water reuse, wind power with solar panels, and into which house he would one day install his environmentally conscious bride and raise a large, organically-fed, happy family (*Note: Make the family "realistically" happy; throw in some eating issues for the daughter, whose body dysmorphic disorder will vanish after a heart-to-heart talk and a dad-to-daughter-appropriate hug on the wrap-around porch in the cool Vermont air one night, as her mother watches this exchange, unobserved, peeking from behind an organic linen curtain.*)

But wherein how, one day, last fall, reality invaded Jessica's life. For when she least expected it, that was when Jessica Henry met The Carpenter! Well, not The *Carpenter*-Carpenter. And not at the food co-op either, but at a four-week (one hour per week) CPR and AED certification class that she enrolled in at Saint Vincent's Hospital, playing with the idea of quitting her receptionist job and becoming both an EMT and a fiction writer, believing that experience with bodies and blood and life and death might help lend some gravitas to her writing. And wherein how also registered as a student in this CPR class would be a "real life" carpenter (or, more precisely, a man who works with tools) just like the "fantasy-based" (Tina's term) Carpenter. Except not exactly. The man who worked with tools was not quite as tall as she'd fantasized. And his hair didn't undulate because there was no hair: he had a shaved head—but around that head he wore what looked to Jessica to be a hemp bandana. His body was youthful and lithe and strong; Jessica kept looking at the sinews of muscle in his neck and forearms. And he had that certain type of slightly not-handsome handsome face and soul-penetrating eyes that made it difficult for Jessica to look at without feeling a little lost. In other words, he was hot. And wherein how this hot "real life" carpenter was named Cal Hagarty, and how Cal Hagarty would be taking the CPR class because both his brother and his father were fire fighters, and, well, he guessed also because his hours were recently cut back at his job at Home Depot, and he had felt like . . . well, he guessed he just should know CPR, everybody should know CPR, he guessed. Which frank, insightful, and vulnerable admission he shared with everyone on the first night of the class when they went around classroom B-16 (located in a dim and dank part of the basement) doing introductions, and which admission was nearly perfectly transcribed in

Jessica's Moleskine journal. And yet Jessica Henry did not hear another introduction (including her own, which went something like, "I'm Jessica, and I'm just really interested in the possibility of saving lives.") because she was already composing in her mind the rest of Cal Hagarty's story: Wherein how Cal Hagarty had wanted to take this CPR class not to compete with his fire fighter family, but in order to gain lifesaving skills that would ready him for an emergency after he had installed his new bride and had started his young family in the wild and unpredictable landscape of Vermont, a landscape beautiful and romantic, but disproportionately low in numbers of EMTs, and if something were ever to happen to his beautiful, artistic wife or to their realistically happy children he would now be trained in the ways of saving them. And wherein how (as Jessica was now imagining this scenario) at the end of the evening of that first CPR class, Cal would ask Jessica if she would be his partner for the upcoming partner-portion of the course, in which he and she might have to practice mouth-to-mouth or perhaps just touch each other's bodies in vital places for reasons of lifesaving and/or survival—pulses and cleared passageways and checking orifices and whatnot.

And wherein how, in reality, although they never kissed, much less touched mouths or vital body parts or inspected orifices (there was a head-and-torso mannequin everyone practiced on), and wherein how even though in reality she and Cal didn't even talk in that first class (the teacher—a red-headed nurse who every time she knelt or bent over the mannequin, Jessica could see her black lace bra and her frankly *intimidating* cleavage—assigned partners herself, and Cal Hagarty ended up working with her), Jessica Henry nonetheless could not stop thinking about

Cal that night while riding home on the subway. Some full-on dissociative fantasizing right there on the F train, careening toward Queens, toward Jackson Heights, toward Rupa and Morgana and goddess knew who else. But wherein how later that night at her apartment, weirdly, even though things did not go as she had fantasized they would go with Cal, she was nonetheless able to fall asleep easily for the first time in what seemed like forever despite Rupa and Sanjay's arguing and Morgana's wall-thumping sex, able to fall asleep without her usual dosage of Ambien and internet-acquired Lendormin, which she would swallow with Budweiser, afterwards breaking Rupa's "number one" apartment rule by smoking out her bedroom window. Jessica found she was able to fall asleep by merely thinking about Cal Hagarty, focusing on the idea of Cal. And that was something even The Carpenter had not been able to do—conquer her insomnia. And so she understood now—not without a bit of mourning and nostalgia—that the time had come to say goodbye to The Carpenter. Time to leave The Carpenter, and cleave to Cal.

And wherein how for the next couple of weeks, before drifting naturally to sleep, Jessica would lie in bed, sober, well-rested, musing on all things Cal, twirling her curls in her fingers, her old Raggedy Andy doll on her chest, where he always slept. In her favorite scenario, she and Cal would be attending the CPR class's graduation, wearing their CPR cap and gowns and their disposable safety face shields, and Cal would hold Jessica's hand the entire time and ignore the teacher, and yet she (the teacher) would seem to accept her loss of Cal and nod affirmingly and respectfully, albeit defeatedly, at Jessica, as if to say, "The best woman won." And Jessica would grin and feel swoony and giddy and grip Cal's hand tighter, and then she and Cal would be back at her apartment on her bed, having sex, and she enjoyed it, swoony and giddy and getting into it. And Cal, getting into it too, would begin to wallop her pelvically against her headboard and Jessica enjoyed that too, moaning and encouraging Cal to wallop harder, and then Cal was moaning louder and walloping and someone was shouting and then they were both moaning and walloping, Jessica doing her best to meet his pelvic thrusts with her own thrusts, a pelvic call-and-response. Moaning and walloping and pelvically calling and responding. Shouts and bangs and then Morgana's actual real-life wall-thumping woke her, and Jessica realized it had been a dream. But instead of experiencing her usual anger and subsequent despair, she felt elated that she had been able to fall asleep at all, and she let the idea of Cal come forward again and reduce those domestic annoyances to a barely noticeable level. Cal was her savior. Jessica slept.

And wherein, for next few weeks, safe in such repose, Jessica had an epiphany. (Note: Careful of "unearned" e's.) Her new-found awareness of Cal's "real" saving grace brought with it a call to action. Enough with the fantasy world already, enough with imaginary carpenters. Cal was not a dream, but a real man in her real world. And so she knew she needed to *make a move*, needed to tell Cal how she felt about him. But the time was nigh. There was only one more CPR class left! (Note: Watch what wksp bitch called "hysterical punctuation in order to heighten suspense.") And wherein she decided that at the next (and last!) CPR class she would tell the real Cal Hagarty in real life her real feelings.

And so, wherein, on the night of the last CPR class, after pinning back her hair and outlining her eyes and wearing her black faux-leather boots and her flapper skirt and her grandmother's faux-fur coat, she set off for the glittering island of Manhattan, toward her CPR class—and her destiny! Her loosely-sketched plan was to sit in the seat next to the seat that Cal always sat in (the one next to the teacher's desk), and then try to catch his eye and smile at him at some point during the class, and then talk to him when class was over. So far that was all the plan she had. Yet that was enough. But she had to hurry because Cal was always the first to arrive to class, always sitting there, his eyes cast down at the floor, spinning his pen in his fingers when Jessica entered room B-16. Thus she needed to get there before he did so it wouldn't look like any of this had been planned. If she appeared in any way obvious, she knew she'd lose her nerve. She left her apartment with fifty-five minutes to go until class. Plenty of time. However, when she got to her subway station at Roosevelt Avenue, the F train to Manhattan wasn't running! Some police action in Times Square! The dark blue MTA workers suggesting alternate routes. And so she had to suffer, minute by minute, through a sluggish and over-crowded R train ride making all local stops to Union Square—nearly a mile from Saint Vincent's!—her knee bouncing and foot tapping the whole time, her eyes scanning the dark, many-face-reflected window.

She emerged from Union Square with only twenty minutes until class started. But she felt calm. The November air in New York City that evening reminded her of the time long ago when she first saw the boy across the tracks. And Jessica thought how far she'd come from that insecure girl at Gallows Hill High afraid to cross the tracks to talk to a boy. She was a writer now and an EMT in training. She could de-fib and cauterize. She could narrate in first-person and close third. Sure, there were still some challenges: hypodermic needles took some practice, as did stream-of-consciousness. But, regardless, she had come so far from that city of crones. She was now a cosmopolitan woman, a citizen of the world. She crossed Sixth Avenue on 12th Street with fifteen minutes remaining. She would have to sit in some other seat, but, so what, nothing could stop her now.

When she got off the elevator in the basement of Saint Vincent's, she could see down the hall that the lights were already on in classroom B-16, and she could hear some students chatting. Still five minutes left until class. No time for second thoughts. She slowed her pace and took a deep breath. It was then she heard a noise in a classroom to the right just ahead of her. When she reached the door, she looked inside, and then stopped. There was Cal with his back to the door, standing at a big wooden desk, leaning on it. Jessica could see the blue billow of his boxer shorts puffing out over the back of his jeans. The EMT teacher-nurse was sitting on top of the desk. Cal had one of his hands around her neck, holding it the way someone would hold an apple they were getting ready to bite. And then the teacher's hand came up around Cal's back and slipped into his blue underwear. And then Jessica wasn't exactly standing anymore; she was listing, teetering, trying to lean away from the door frame and keep out of sight, but actually she was falling, and so she let the weight of her body assist her in spinning to the left, like a silent-film actress affecting a safe swoon to the stage floor. Jessica's boot seemed stuck on the uneven concrete, and in what felt like slow-motion she went down. It all seemed to be taking place as if in some weak, washed-out watercolor painting. The overhead fluorescent lights were nonetheless dim in the corridor under the hospital, and two broken wheelchairs sat bumped up against a yellow rubber barrel. She sat there, on the cold floor, in a small pile of coat and bent legs and spread skirt and splayed palms, seeming to shrink down as though being digested into those layers, disappearing into all that faux-material, like the Wicked Witch after Dorothy's dousing.

And wherein how Jessica Henry actually gathered enough of herself to stand up and make it into classroom B-16 before Cal and the teacher arrived (separately, of course: Cal first, his eyes cast down; and then she, a head and torso carried under her arm). Jessica sat through that last class—oblivious, vibrating, jittery, detached, *dissociated*, starving, empty, hungerless, cold, sullen, lost. She called on The Carpenter, but now he was lost too. And though she tried everything to resuscitate and save the carpenter, she couldn't bring him back to life. And wherein Jessica Henry had a despairing realization going home on the F train after that final CPR class (for which there actually was no graduation, just a few people who went out for drinks, but who did not invite Jessica to join them). She realized that she never had a chance with Cal Hagarty, and would never have a chance with him. And a part of her didn't care. But another part throbbed for him. If she had only talked to him that very first night . . . but then, in reality, she knew that never would have happened. Never would've happened because she was what she was: an ugly, tedious, ridiculous, embarrassing, fearful daughter of a cellar-dweller. Forget being persecuted; she was that worst of all things: *unnoticed*.

And wherein how there were now days when she was not able to get out of bed or go to work or leave her bedroom or even eat. And wherein how when she experienced this debilitating soul sickness, she would lie in bed on her side fetally wrapped around a pillow and rocking slowly, with eyes closed, moaning Cal Hagarty's name over and over, like a prayer, like an incantation, until she fell asleep. And wherein how on some particularly intense nights of soul-sickening psychic pain, after falling asleep in this incantatory way, she would half-way wake up after midnight with the light still on with the word *Cal* coming off her lips, which wasn't even a clearly annunciated *Cal* but more like a low murmur of *Cal* issuing forth like breath from her barely moving mouth, again and again and again it issued, over and over, ceaseless and indomitable, like the tide, as she swam up and out over those waves and back into deeper waters, aware on some level that with each utterance of *Cal* her top lip would turn up a little and her eyes would squinch at their corners as though she were in pain. And she could feel this expression continue to form on her face as she repeated Cal's name, but not now as a pain-*reliever*, but, rather, as a pain-*reminder*. *(Note: Maybe change title of story from "The Carpenter" to "Remembrance of Pain Past" or to some obscure Latin term that would lend the story a quality of classical tragedy.)* And wherein exactly how and why she would want to be reminded of such pain she couldn't understand, but she was aware that this squinchy-faced, lip-curled *Cal*-moan was almost the same facial expression and same sound she made as when she would rub with all four fingers her clit to come, saying with each circular swipe of her fingers, *Cal, Cal, Cal, Cal*, and making the same squinchy face—but one now not of psychic pain and unnameable loneliness and soul-sickening depression, but one of *intense erotic pleasure*. And wherein how even to her half-conscious mind she understood that that facial expression of erotic pleasure was identical to the expression of psychic anguish; it could, in fact, to an objective observer appear to be the *exact same face.* Anyone merely observing her would find it difficult to know exactly how or what she was feeling, find it difficult to distinguish between Jessica Henry's expressions of pain and those of erotic pleasure, which she made when making herself come murmuring *Cal,* her four fingers pushing down and moving in rapid circles as though she were trying to rub a genie from a bottle.

And wherein how when the motion of her hand would finally slow down, Jessica would lay spent, returned from her orgasm back to the anguish-ridden world, a world whose hard edges and cold surfaces and loud knockings reasserted themselves as she regained the sensations of her body on the damp-sheeted bed. And wherein how regaining these sensations in a "real world" without Cal Hagarty anywhere near her was itself such an intense anguish that she could hardly endure the experience without beginning to make small animal noises into her pillow. And wherein how this Cal-less world's psychic anguish would then force her to roll over again, back onto her side and wrap herself fetally once more around a pillow and—still damp-genitaled, still dewy-fingered—moan the word *Cal* over and over again as she yet once more suffered herself to sleep. And wherein how at that exact moment in that horrible year, there would be no mistaking Jessica Henry's squinchy face of anguish for anything but pure anguish—horrible, horrible anguish; nothing there even remotely resembling erotic pleasure now, nothing that anyone would even believe was possible for any human to feel, especially such an underdeveloped character as Jessica Henry. *Not believable,* they'd comment. *She never even talked to the guy,* they'd comment. *Emotionally unconvincing,* they'd comment. A failed attempt at fiction, they'd say, a failure from beginning to end. A horrible piece of work. Nothing that anyone would care about or believe or have any desire to read—if, that is, she were ever to write this story.

Acknowledgments

Grateful acknowledgement is made to the editors of the following publications, where these stories appeared in slightly different form:

Dossier Journal: "Late Thaw";
H.O.W. Journal: "Parts";
LIT: "Annus Horribilis, or The Carpenter, or Cal";
New York Tyrant: "Man on Couch";
Open City: "Practice Problem";
Post Road: "Unheimliche";
Salt Hill: "Everlovin'";
Sleeping Fish: "The Subjunctive Mood";
Willow Springs: "Reduction";
110 Stories: New York Writes after September 11th (NYU Press): "Post Card".

Thanks to Debra Anderson, Caroline Berger, John Brown, Rebbecca Brown, Blake Butler, Peter Conners, Andrew Cotto, Rachel Heiman, Leah Iannone, Rod Kessler, Katherine Krause, Samuel Ligon, Robert Lopez, Brent McDonald, Jen McDonald, Angela Patrinos, Robert Polito, Devin Poore and the whole Altered Fluids crew, Matthew Vollmer, and Andrew Zornoza.

About the Author

Joseph Salvatore has published fiction and criticism in *The Brooklyn Rail*, *Dossier Journal*, *H.O.W. Journal*, *LIT*, *New York Tyrant*, *Open City*, *Post Road*, *Salt Hill*, *Sleeping Fish*, *Willow Springs*, *110 Stories* (NYU Press, 2001), and *Routledge's Encyclopedia of Queer Culture* (2003). He is a regular fiction reviewer for *The New York Times Book Review*, and an assistant professor at The New School, where he founded their literary journal, *LIT*, and was awarded the University's Award for Teaching Excellence. He lives in New York.

BOA Editions, Ltd.
American Reader Series

Colophon

To Assume a Pleasing Shape, stories by Joseph Salvatore, is set in Mrs. Eaves, a typeface designed in 1996 by Zuzana Licko (1961–) and named after Sarah Eaves. Originally John Baskerville's live-in housekeeper, she became his mistress and eventually married him after her estranged husband, Richard Eaves, died. She worked alongside Baskerville in his printing business in Birmingham, England, and completed the volumes remaining after his death in 1775.

The publication of this book is made possible, in part, by the special support of the following individuals:

Anonymous

Liz Axelrod

Joseph Belluck, *in honor of Bernadette Catalana*

Pete & Bev French

Anne Germanacos ❖ Suzanne Gouvernet

Robin, Hollon & Casey Hursh, *in memory of Peter Hursh*

X. J. Kennedy

Katy Lederer

Deborah Ronnen & Sherman Levey

Rosemary & Lew Lloyd

Janice N. Harrington & Robert Dale Parker

Angela Patrinos

Mr. & Mrs. Karl W. Postler

Boo Poulin

Steven O. Russell & Phyllis Rifkin-Russell

Melissa Hall & Joe Torre ❖ Ellen & David Wallack

Dan & Nan Westervelt, *in honor of Pat Braus & Ed Lopez*

Glenn & Helen William